ARMANDO

DI SALVO CRIME FAMILY
BOOK THREE

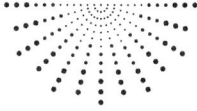

CAMERON HART

WANT A FREE BOOK?

Sign up for my newsletter and get your copy of Chasing Stacy.

River: One look at the stunning waitress carrying the weight of the world on her shoulders, and I'm a gonner. I wasn't looking for a sweet little thing with auburn hair and more baggage than I can fit on the back of my bike, but there's no going back now. She's mine. I'll prove to her I'm more than capable of handling her past and making her feel safe again.

CONNECT WITH ME!

Check out my website, cameronhart.net, for sneak previews on my latest projects.

Follow me on social media:
  Facebook Page
  Facebook Group
  TikTok
  Instagram
  Goodreads
  Bookbub

ARMANDO

I was obsessed with the blue-eyed pixie from the second she jumped into my arms. Allegra. She clung to me and prayed for me to keep her safe, just for a little while. Allegra had just escaped from her degenerate uncle, and she had no idea she ran straight into a mafia enforcer.

I've always been proud of my position within the Di Salvo family, but I'm not sure someone as sweet and innocent as Allegra will understand. For the first time, I wonder if my profession will keep me from the one thing I want most in life.

With threats both old and new, and everyone in the Di Salvo family on edge, it's only a matter of time before the truth comes out. Will my sweet girl be able to forgive me?

CHAPTER ONE

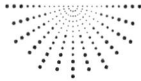

ARMANDO

"**G**ood morning, what can I get for... Oh."

I give the barista my most charming smile, but the hesitancy in her eyes doesn't dim. I get it. I'm six foot eight, nearly three hundred pounds of pure muscle, with ink crawling up and down my arms. I stand out anywhere, but especially in this dainty little coffee shop.

"Morning, miss," I greet her, hoping to put the little lady at ease. I might make a living off of my intimidating size and looks, but I don't enjoy frightening civilians unnecessarily. Strange, I know, considering I'm an enforcer for the most powerful mafia family in New York, the Di Salvos.

"Uh, right. Yes. What can I get for you?" the woman asks, avoiding eye contact.

"Double shot, please. I need it this morning."

She types out my order and takes my money, thanking me when I hand her a twenty and tell her to keep the change. I walk to the other side of the counter to wait for my drink, taking a spot in the back so as not to block the way of the other patrons. They all part for me like the Red Sea, shuffling out of the way to clear a path.

I've gotten used to people staring at me or making a point *not* to stare at me. I hit the six-foot mark by the time I was fourteen, which helped me out in a lot of ways since I looked much older than I was. Specifically, when I was looking for an escape from the torture that is the American foster care system.

I hit the streets shortly after my fourteenth birthday with nothing except for my best friend and what I could fit in a backpack. Leif and I looked after each other, and even though our lives took drastically different turns, he's still my oldest and closest friend.

As soon as Leif turned eighteen, he enlisted in the military. They gave him food, shelter, training, and a purpose— all things we lacked in our lives. I went in a different direction. When I turned eighteen, I also had an opportunity to join something bigger than myself—the Mafia.

Leif still doesn't understand, but I don't expect him to. Especially now that the bastard has found himself a woman after all these years. Never thought I'd see the day, but Maribell is just what he needs. After he was wounded overseas, there were some dark times. I was there during the surgeries and most of the healing process, but his wounds were far more than skin deep.

I couldn't help my friend out of his depression or even begin to understand what living with PTSD must have been like for him. But Maribell waltzed into his life and eased his pain.

I'm happy for him. Truly, no one deserves a happily ever after more than Leif, especially after everything he's been through. I'd be lying if I said I wasn't a little jealous. Not of Maribell, specifically, but just having someone. Caring for someone. Being the most important person in someone's life and doing whatever it takes to keep them safe and happy.

"Double shot for Armando," the lady calls from behind the counter, startling me from my thoughts.

Jesus, I'm losing it. When did I become a sappy fool? Maybe something is in the water. Not only did Leif settle down with a woman, but the big Boss himself, Romeo, found the love of his life. And even more shockingly, the cold, aloof underboss of the family, Dante, also fell ass over heels for a woman last week.

It's a lot of change all at once. Staring down the barrel of my fortieth birthday has me feeling some kind of way about the life I've built. Don't get me wrong, I'm proud of my rank within the Di Salvos, and I've worked my ass off to get to where I am today. I went from sleeping in a cardboard box under an overpass in the South Bronx to living in a three-story, five-bedroom, three-bathroom house with a gym and home theater in the basement. By all accounts, I've made it to the top.

There's just one thing missing—someone to share it with.

Clearing my throat, I rub the heel of my hand over my chest to ease the tension there. I step up to the counter and grab my drink, downing it in ten seconds. The liquid burns my throat, both from the temperature and the acidity. That's how I know it's good espresso.

I set the tiny mug in the dirty dish tub before making my way to the exit. It's just past ten in the morning, and that was just the pick-me-up I needed to get me through the rest of the day. This afternoon, I have meetings with the Boss and Dante, his number two, which isn't my favorite activity. I'd rather be out on a mission, using my strength for the good of the family.

Still, Romeo is constantly reminding me that this job is more than just throwing our weight around. It's about strategy too. That's always been more of Dante's wheelhouse than mine, but I'm trying to be more open. It might just kill me.

I open the door of the coffee shop, holding it for an older couple on their way inside. As soon as I step onto the sidewalk, a flash of light red catches my eye, and I turn my head to see a petite woman sprinting toward me, her long, strawberry-blonde hair flowing behind her as she picks up speed. I swear she's about to run right into...

The woman's bright blue eyes latch onto mine, a look of fear and desperation emanating from them. The next second, she collides into my chest, wrapping her arms around my neck and clinging to me with every ounce of strength she has.

"I'm sorry," she murmurs, her voice scratchy and broken. "Please," the woman whispers, tears clogging her throat as she buries her head between my neck and shoulder. "Please just... I just... I'm sorry." My chest caves in at her words, and I hold her close, not sure what drove her into my arms, but knowing with absolute certainty I will destroy whatever and whoever made her feel like this.

"Are you in danger?" I ask, though I already know the answer. The woman sniffles and nods against my shoulder. "Running from a bad man?" Again, she nods, a shiver wracking her body, which I'm trying not to ogle. It's nearly impossible when her curves are pressed against me, her softness melting into the hard slats of my muscles.

I carry the trembling, terrified woman back inside the coffee shop, hoping to hide her from whoever is chasing her down. Ignoring the curious and shocked glances, I stride through the seating area until I find a booth along the back wall. It will give us some privacy while I figure out who this gorgeous, frightened woman is and how I can help her.

Setting her down on her feet, I guide the woman to sit in the booth. She nearly collapses, but I keep her hand in mine, easing her into the seat. I'm about to grab some napkins from the counter to dry her tears, but as soon as I try to withdraw my hand, she grips it tighter, a heart-shattering whimper falling from her lips.

Kneeling in front of her, I look up into her clear blue eyes, rimmed in red and watery from crying. She sears me with a look of pure sorrow mixed with helplessness. Without knowing a single thing about this woman, I understand her more than she could possibly imagine.

"S-sorry," she stutters out, blinking away more tears. "I don't… I don't… I didn't know what to do."

"It's okay," I say softly, rubbing the pad of my thumb over her knuckles in what I hope is a soothing gesture.

She's silent for a few moments, and I encourage her to take a few deep breaths. She's shivering from head to toe, and I notice for the first time that her shirt is ripped. It's a V-neck with some logo I don't recognize, and it's far too tight for her ample chest. It looks like someone grabbed the hem to keep her from escaping, resulting in a good-sized tear up one side.

My gaze wanders up her arms, pausing to examine the dark bruises on her wrists and biceps. *What the fuck has she been through?* Rage rolls over me in waves, my adrenaline spiking once more at the thought of some motherfucker's grubby hands on this precious woman.

"I just s-saw you and knew you were big enough to p-protect me."

"I am. I will," I vow. I've never meant anything more in my entire life. She's tied to me now. I can't explain it, and I don't want to. I need to get her to safety. We'll figure everything else out from there. "What's your name?"

Her cheeks flush a light shade of pink, making her glow even as she's falling apart in front of me. "Allegra," she murmurs, tucking some of her hair behind her ear. She gives me the smallest of smiles, and Jesus Christ, I can hardly breathe when she looks at me like that.

"Allegra," I repeat, committing each syllable to memory. I like the way it rolls off my tongue. "I'm Armando," I tell her, lifting her hand already clasped in mine and shaking it.

Another hint of a smile lights up her face, but it's soon replaced by a nervous, desperate anxiousness.

"Can I get you some tea? Something to calm your nerves? Or maybe a muffin? They have great coffee cake here too."

Allegra shakes her head no, then drops her gaze. "I don't have any money," she whispers. "I don't have... anything. I don't have *anything*." She blinks a few times as if the reality of her situation is dawning on her. "I don't have anything," she repeats, her bottom lip quivering.

"Hey now," I say in what I hope is a calming voice. "That's not true. You have me."

I hoped to make her feel safe and protected like she asked, but the terrified woman muffles a sob as tears stream down her cheeks. Seeing her in this kind of agony is excruciating, and without thinking, I pull her into my lap.

Allegra curls up against me, burying her head into my neck. I cup her head, keeping her close as I wrap my other arm around her back, pressing her further into my embrace.

"I've got you," I murmur, running the tips of my fingers up and down her spine in soothing strokes. "I don't know what you're running from, but you picked the right person to protect you."

Allegra nods, settling something deep in my soul. On some level, she knows she's safe with me. It's a start.

I push down the crazy, possessive thoughts of her going to someone else for help. They could have taken advantage of her situation. They could have hurt her worse than she already is.

"Everyone is staring at us," she whispers, her body growing stiff in my arms. "I'm making a scene."

"I'll pluck their eyes out if it will make you feel better," I half-joke. She has no idea what lengths I'd go to in order to keep her comfortable. I'm already obsessed with her, and I'm not sure what to do about it.

A soft giggle falls from her lips. God, I'm already addicted to it. This woman is going to destroy me.

I can't wait.

CHAPTER TWO

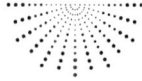

ALLEGRA

I don't know what comes over me, but hearing the handsome man grunt about plucking eyeballs out is hilarious. A laugh bubbles up from some hidden reservoir as this stranger holds me in his arms.

A million thoughts race through my mind as my laughter turns into something else. Something manic. Unhinged, almost. I hear myself laugh and then choke on a sob, but it doesn't feel real. It doesn't feel like my body or my voice.

"I've got you," Armando whispers again, cupping my face. "You're safe now. Look at me." He wipes away my tears with the pad of his thumb, guiding me to face him. "That's it, sweetheart," he says softly. "I'm right here, and I'm going to get you through this."

I want to protest, to tell him he shouldn't get involved with me and that I'm not worth the trouble, but the words die on my tongue when his hazel eyes meet mine. They're filled with understanding and surprising tenderness, and the longer I stare into their depths, the warmer I feel.

He's surrounding me with his strength and presence, but it's not suffocating like so many other men in my life.

Armando may be nearly double my size, but he's treating me gently like I'm some treasure. Truthfully, I'm the furthest thing from precious. I'm a disaster, and a dangerous one at that. Still, I want to soak up every ounce of peace and safety from Armando while I can.

Armando gives me a small smile, his thumb still stroking my cheek soothingly. What is it about this man? Why did I jump into his arms? After what I've been through, throwing myself at a giant muscular beast probably wasn't my best move. Maybe my self-preservation instincts are broken, which makes a lot of sense.

"I, um…" I trail off, not knowing what I was going to say.

God, I'm such a mess. How did I end up here? *My uncle…*

I slam my eyes shut, unable to even think the words. Shit. I need to get out of here. I need to move far, far away, and disappear. Go off the grid. He has connections all over the city, and the longer I stay here, the more time I'm giving him to track me.

Fuck. *Fuck.*

I attempt to scramble off the kind stranger's lap, but he draws me further into his comforting embrace.

"Are you okay?" he whispers.

"Yes," I answer automatically. I'm always okay. What other choice do I have? It's not like anyone cares.

"You should wait a few seconds next time someone asks you that," he says. I lean back enough to give him a questioning look. "If you answer too quickly, they'll know you're lying. Give it a moment or two before settling on an answer. Take it from someone who faked being *okay* for a long time."

I blink at the man before me, unsure what to do with that information. He clears his throat and averts his gaze as if embarrassed at his confession. It endears him to me, knowing he put himself out there to make me feel better.

"Thank you," I murmur, nibbling on my bottom lip. "I…

I'm not okay, truthfully," I add. "But it's not something for you to worry about. It's no one's problem but my own."

This time, when I untangle myself from Armando, he lets me. I know it's irrational, but a pang of disappointment echoes in my chest. I thought maybe this man would fight to keep me pressed against him, but that's absurd.

As soon as I stand, Armando joins me. "Where are we going, angel?" he asks, a smile curling up the corner of his lips.

I didn't get a good look at him before jumping into his arms. I knew he was tall, but holy crap. Armando has to be over a foot taller than me. His shoulders are so wide and muscular that I'm surprised he can fit through doorways. Coupled with sharp features and a perpetual five-o'clock shadow, he's the kind of man I should be afraid of, the kind of man I *am* afraid of, but with Armando...

It's his eyes—golden brown with a hint of green. Buried underneath layers of beautiful colors, his eyes hold something gentle. Something fragile that I want to protect.

Crazy, I know. I'm not making any sense, but then again, this whole day isn't making one bit of goddamn sense. Who can I trust? Not my family, not my friends, not my co-workers, so why not this man? He's done more for me in the last ten minutes than anyone else has in the previous twenty-one years of my life.

"Allegra?" he prompts softly when I still haven't answered. "Do you have anywhere to stay?"

"Yeah, of course," I lie. Armando raises an eyebrow, calling me out. "I mean, I will. As soon as I call a shelter." Looking away from his golden-brown gaze, shame creeps up my spine and winds around my lungs until it's hard to breathe.

Here he is, tall, chiseled, handsome, and kind, wearing an expensive suit, shiny shoes, and what looks to be a very pricey watch. I'm homeless, jobless, and truly alone in this world. I have nothing and no one. How pathetic is that?

"Breathe for me, sweetheart," Armando whispers, gathering my hand up and placing it on his chest. He inhales deeply, nodding as I do the same. I didn't realize how shallow my breathing had become. We exhale slowly, and his heart beats reassuringly beneath my palm. It grounds me in a way I don't understand. "Good. Again," he murmurs.

Hazel eyes meet mine, pulling me closer, tethering my soul to his. The crashing waves of anxiety slowly recede, and I'm no longer drowning in terror.

"Now," Armando continues, his gaze never leaving mine. "How about I take you back to my place? You can wash up, get some food and water, and take a nap."

"No, that's too much," I deflect, stepping back. "I need to get away from here. Can you drop me off at a bus station?" My mind starts spinning again when I remember I don't have anything with me. No cash, no phone, no ID, nothing. "I'll pay you back for the ticket once I get set up…" I trail off, knowing I have no future and no way to make money.

"We'll take it one step at a time. You don't have to plan everything out right now. Just take the next step."

"I don't even know what the next step is," I admit softly, dipping my head.

Armando lifts my chin with the crook of his finger and tucks a lock of hair behind my ear. "Do you trust me, Allegra?"

My instant reaction is *yes*, though that's quickly followed by, *oh, fuck no.*

"I… I want to," I answer honestly.

"I can work with that," he says with a soft smile. "Step one is letting me take care of you, just for tonight. We can reassess in the morning."

"But…"

"I have more than enough room. You'll have a room with an en suite bathroom. Locks on both doors, and I'll understand if you want to go straight to your room and lock me out. It will be your safe space, and I'll only enter if you give me permission."

"But..."

"And I have a giant lasagna made by my friend's fiancée yesterday, so you'd be helping me by emptying my fridge."

"But..."

"Clothes! I can get you clothes. Girly shit. Whatever you need."

Armando looks frazzled, like he's trying to come up with a way to provide everything for me right here and now. The only question I have is...

"Why?"

Armando stares at me for a moment, studying the very depths of my being. I feel raw and vulnerable, yet seen and understood.

"Because someone did the same for me when I was in a similar situation," he whispers, cupping my cheek. "You don't know this yet, Allegra, but life isn't supposed to be this hard. I don't know your story, but I've seen enough to know you were dealt a bad hand. Let me help. Let me make up for how you've been treated for so long."

I blink back tears, not comprehending the man standing before me. Is he really this kind? This caring of a stranger who jumped into his arms and begged for protection?

"Okay," I hear myself say.

"Okay?" he repeats, sounding shocked and excited at the same time. It's kind of adorable.

I nod, slipping my hand into his. Armando wraps his fingers around my hand, tucking me into his side as we walk to the back of the coffee shop.

"I texted my driver to pull around to the alley. More coverage that way. I can keep you safe."

I want to ask what he does for a living. He clearly has a lot of money, and now I find out he has a personal driver. We'll have time to talk about that stuff later. Right now, I'm having a hard time putting one foot in front of the other.

"I've got you," Armando murmurs, scooping me into his arms once we're outside.

"I can walk," I protest weakly.

"And I can carry you," he counters, looking at me with that grin I'm starting to love.

He sets me down in front of the car, opens the back door, and crawls in behind me. Armando gives the driver a quick nod before focusing on me. His arm rests on the back of the seat, and I automatically scoot closer, sighing with relief when he bundles me further into his side.

Resting my head on his shoulder, I breathe in his cedar and spice scent as my heavy eyelids close.

The last thing I remember is Armando whispering that I'm safe.

CHAPTER THREE

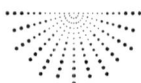

ARMANDO

*T*he angel in my arms stirs as the driver stops outside my home. He moves to get out and open the door for us, but I shake my head, silently letting him know I'll handle it from here.

I look down at my precious cargo, her eyelashes fluttering against her porcelain cheeks the more she wakes up. "You're safe, Allegra," I whisper, knowing she might be disoriented.

"Armando?" she whispers, peeking one eye open.

"Right here," I assure her, giving her a small smile. She relaxes at the sound of my voice, making me feel like the king of the fucking world. My girl trusts me. "Let's get you inside, yeah?"

Allegra nods, regrettably untangling herself from my embrace. I hop out of the car, peering around the front drive and yard for any sign of disturbance. I don't know what the beautiful angel is running from, but I have some powerful enemies of my own to watch out for. Good thing my home is a fortress, and once we're inside, nothing will be able to reach us.

I hold out my hand, and Allegra takes it, clinging to me as I guide her to the front door, which only unlocks with my thumbprint. I make a note to add Allegra's print to the registry. This is her place, too, after all.

Stepping inside, my eyes quickly adjust to the dimmer lighting, and I cringe when I see the dirty dishes from breakfast on the table and counter. I have a few books scattered about and wraps for my knuckles that I use in the gym downstairs. Does it smell funky in here? When was the last time I vacuumed?

I release Allegra's hand and gather the dishes and books, dumping everything onto the counter next to the stove, where they will be mostly hidden until I can clean. Shit. I'll need to grab some cleaning supplies later today. And throw pillows. Women like throw pillows, right? And fuzzy blankets? Candles? I can get that stuff.

After a few moments of tidying up junk mail and dishes, I realize Allegra hasn't spoken a single word. I look through the open kitchen and living room to see her standing inside the door. She hasn't moved an inch, and her arms are wrapped around her torso in a protective hold.

She looks heart-achingly vulnerable as she folds in on herself, her eyes wandering from her dirty clothes and scuffed shoes to my carpet and couch. Allegra stays huddled in the doorway as I take slow steps in her direction so as not to startle her.

"Hey," I say softly. "Sorry about the mess. Please, make yourself at home."

"I'm… I'm gross. I'll make everything gross," she whispers.

Jesus, this girl. She's ripping my heart out with every word. I need to find whoever has her so scared, filled her head with lies, and put their hands on her. Once I have a name, I'll make it my mission to erase them from the face of the earth.

However, Allegra doesn't need that energy from me right now, so I rein it in and focus on the angel before me.

"You're not gross, Allegra. But I understand if you want to rinse the day off. Can I show you your room? It has a bathroom."

She nods, looking up at me with wide, blue eyes. I hold out my hand, loving how Allegra automatically takes it, wrapping her soft fingers around mine.

"You saw the kitchen already," I tell her, nodding in that direction as we stride past the couch and fireplace. "And the living room," I gesture around us. "There's a gym downstairs and a theater if you're into movies."

"You have a theater?" she whispers in bewilderment.

I pause the tour, grinning down at her. "I may have gone a little overboard when I moved in," I admit sheepishly. "I missed out on movies and TV when I was growing up, so I promised myself that when I made it to the top, I'd build a home theater where I could watch anything I wanted. I even have a legit popcorn machine with the butter sauce and everything."

"Really?" Allegra's eyes sparkle with excitement, and I swear to Christ, my heart stops beating in my chest. She's exquisite. Breathtaking. And when she smiles at me, I'm ready to drop to one knee and demand she be mine forever.

I'm out of my damn mind. I know this. But when it comes to Allegra, I don't seem to give a single fuck. I'll need to take it slow with her. She's fragile right now, and the last thing I want is for her to think I'm a creep who only wants one thing from her.

That couldn't be further from the truth. I want *everything* from this girl, and I'll give her all of me in return.

"Really," I finally answer. "I also have connections with

movie studios and can get almost any film sent to me. Even ones not in theaters yet." Am I bragging? A little. I found something my girl is interested in, so hell, yeah, I'm going to go all in.

"What do you do for a living?" she asks. "I mean, you have a beautiful home, a driver, and a theater. You must do well for yourself."

"I, uh…" *Shit.* How can I tell the traumatized angel I beat people up for a living? For the Mafia, no less. She'll think I'm a monster. Hell, I *am* a monster, but I would never hurt her. The thought of harming her makes my stomach churn and acid crawl up my throat.

"Never mind. It's none of my business. I'm sorry. God, that was so rude of me…" Allegra trails off, pulling her hand from mine so she can wrap her arms around her torso.

I hate seeing her like this, and I hate even more that I caused her discomfort. "There's nothing to apologize for," I assure her. "It's true I do well for myself. And I don't mind sharing the spoils."

I give her a wink, which earns me the tiniest smile. I'll take it. I know I need to tell her about my profession eventually, but I hope to have more time to show her I'm more than my job.

I take Allegra's hand again and guide her upstairs to the second room on the right. Opening the door, I step aside to let Allegra look around. She's immediately drawn to the bed, her fingers sliding over the sheets and pillow as if they are the softest things she's ever felt.

My heart clenches in my chest, thinking about where she came from. Did she not have a bed? Blankets? Pillows?

Taking a deep breath, I make a concerted effort to unclench my fists. There will be time to ask questions later. Right now, my woman needs a warm shower, a warm meal, and a warm bed.

"The bathroom is straight through there," I say, pointing to the open door on the east side of the room. "I'll set some clean clothes right outside your door. Take as much time as you need, angel."

Her cheeks flush a gorgeous shade of pink, and it takes everything in me not to pull her into my arms and kiss her. I've never had these intense feelings about anyone before, but I'm not afraid of them. Everything in my life is all or nothing, so it makes sense that love would be the same way.

Holy shit. *Love.*

"Thank you," Allegra murmurs. "For everything. I still don't know why you're being so kind to me. I'm not worth it."

"It kills me to hear you say that. One day you'll see what I see."

Blue eyes latch onto mine, filled with questions. "What do you see?"

"A warrior who has been through hell and back, yet wakes up every day ready to do battle again. That's strength, Allegra. Resilience. I see a woman who has fought for every breath in her lungs and still manages a sweet smile. That's character. Kindness. Selflessness."

"Armando…"

"I know, I know, I'm coming on way too strong. I just–"

"Thank you," she cuts me off, wiping away a tear. "I didn't… I didn't know I needed to hear that. I don't believe everything you said, but I want to live up to that person you described. She sounds incredible."

"*You*, Allegra. You are incredible. I want to help you see that."

Clear blue eyes blink at me before Allegra dips her head, breaking our connection. I need to back off and let her have her space, but it's nearly impossible. Still, I know I gave her a lot to think about. If I want her to trust me, I can't hover over her every second of every day, even if that's exactly what I want to do.

"Come out to the kitchen whenever you're ready. I'll have some food for you."

Allegra nods, and I stand in front of her, unsure if I can leave. Like a dork, I wave at her, then spin on my heel, shaking my head as I make my way to my room.

Once there, I close the door and lean against it, rubbing my hands down my face. My heart is jackhammering against my ribcage, my palms are sweaty, and my mind is racing with a million thoughts and plans.

Right now, I need to focus on one thing at a time. I may be ready to spend the rest of my life with the woman I've only known for half an hour, but she needs time. I'll need to ease her into the idea of forever with a big brute like me.

Filled with a renewed sense of purpose, I dig through my dresser and find a T-shirt, socks, and sweatpants for Allegra. I debate whether to grab a pair of my boxers and ultimately decide to provide everything.

After stacking the neatly folded pile of clothes outside her door, I head to the kitchen and remove the lasagna from the fridge. It's only a few minutes past eleven in the morning, but my girl needs a good home-cooked meal before getting some sleep. I'm not much of a chef, so besides this lasagna Thalia made for me, I only have frozen dinners.

I spend several minutes tidying everything up, frowning at my empty mantle and blank walls. I never realized how lifeless this place is. Even the furniture is generic—I bought the whole set from some fancy store in the Upper East Side after the sales clerk said it was a timeless classic. It was good enough for me at the time, but now I wish I'd gone with something more personal.

It doesn't matter now. Allegra can go on a shopping spree to redecorate. Or, if she doesn't like doing that stuff, I'll give

19

her free rein to hire an interior designer to do it for her. As long as she's happy.

The water from the shower shuts off, snapping me from my thoughts. I try not to picture Allegra stepping out of the shower completely naked, droplets of water cascading down her dips and curves…

Stop it, I scold myself.

Returning to the kitchen, I cut out an enormous slice of lasagna and put it on a plate to warm up in the microwave. I can't stop my foot from tap-tapping nervously against the tiled floor in anticipation of Allegra's presence.

As if conjuring her up, Allegra pads down the hall and appears in the kitchen doorway. She pauses, leaning against the wall as if uncertain of her next steps. I want to pull her into my arms but stay back, letting her come to me.

"Hey," I say softly. "How was the shower?"

"Amazing. Thank you," she whispers.

Allegra takes a few tentative steps into the kitchen, and I register what she's wearing. Goddamn, I like seeing her in my T-shirt, which hangs down to her knees. She doesn't have the sweatpants on, and I'm guessing it's because she was drowning in them. I don't mind. Allegra has my socks pulled halfway up her shins, and she's so fucking adorable I don't know what to do with myself.

I hold out my hand, watching as the tension drains from her shoulders. She gives me a smile and closes the distance between us, taking my hand. I study her face, noticing the freckles on her nose and cheeks for the first time. I notice something else for the first time, too. A deep horizontal scar on the right side of her neck. It's nearly an inch thick and four inches long.

Allegra gasps softly and drops my hand, immediately covering up the scar. "Sorry," she murmurs.

"Stop apologizing for everything, sweetheart."

Allegra nods, but her shoulders curl in, and she's doing her best to hide from me.

"Look at me, Allegra."

She takes a cleansing breath and raises her head, meeting my gaze again.

"Good girl."

Shit, where did that come from?

I'm about to apologize, but then I see something flash in her eyes. Fuck me. She likes it. I can't think about that right now. I have more important things to deal with.

"Don't hide from me," I murmur. "Scars are nothing to be ashamed of. They prove you survived."

Keeping my eyes locked on hers, I lift the hem of my shirt to reveal a similar-sized scar crawling up my left side.

Allegra's eyes widen, and she reaches out to place her hand over my skin, stopping when she's a millimeter away. "Does it hurt?"

"Not anymore."

Allegra presses her hand against the raised skin as if her touch alone could heal me. She has no idea that's exactly what she's doing. I rest my hand over hers, leaning down and brushing my lips against the shell of her ear.

"You're beautiful," I breathe. "You survived. You're here. And you're safe."

She surprises me by throwing her arms around my waist and burying her head in my chest. "This has to be a dream," I hear her say. "You can't be real."

I hold her close, resting one hand on her lower back while the other strokes up and down her spine.

"I thought the same thing about you," I tell her truthfully.

Allegra loosens her hold and leans back slightly to give me a questioning look. Before I can respond, my phone rings. Allegra squeaks and jumps back while I curse.

"Sorry, sweetheart," I apologize, hating how jumpy she is.

21

It's a testament to everything she's been through. Romeo's name flashes across the screen, and I know I need to check in for the day. "I have to take this. There's a huge slice of lasagna in the microwave. Just heat it up for a few minutes, and you should be good to go."

Reluctantly, I step away from the beautiful, broken angel and silence my phone before it rings again. "Make yourself at home," I tell her as I gather my things. "I'll be back in a few hours."

Allegra nods and waves from the kitchen as I open the front door. I want to kiss her, promise her ridiculous things, and proclaim my love for her, but it's all too fast.

Instead of doing any of those crazy things, I wave back and smile, counting down the minutes until I can return home to my woman.

CHAPTER FOUR

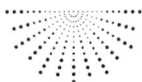

ALLEGRA

I roll over and snuggle into the softest, warmest bed I've ever slept in.

And then it hits me.

I don't own a bed.

Panic punctures my lungs, and I struggle to breathe as I try to remember how I got here. *Did someone drug me? Knock me out? Did my uncle sell me off to the highest bidder like he's always threatening?*

My stomach churns violently at the thought, and I sit up, hoping to get a better idea of the threat I'm dealing with. Swinging my legs over the side of the bed, bits and pieces of the last few hours filter into my mind.

I was running, running, running, looking for somewhere safe to hide, and then...

Armando.

He held me in his arms, his warmth and strength radiating from him as he carried me inside. Closing my eyes, I remember his gentle touch and kind words as he talked me through the most traumatic moments of my life.

More of the day plays out in my head. Armando convinced me to stay with him. I took a hot shower, and then he fed me. We shared a moment in the kitchen. I lift my hand to my neck and run my fingers over the marred skin.

Armando saw my brutal scar and showed me his. He'll never understand how much that meant to me. He looked at the ugliest part of me and didn't back down. The man doesn't even know me, yet he revealed a vulnerable part of himself to comfort me.

I have no idea why Armando is being so patient and kind. I leaped into his arms and clung to him like a spider monkey, but he can't be doing all of this out of some misplaced obligation, right? Most people would have shrugged me off or, if they were half-decent, given me a ride to the nearest shelter.

Wiping away my tears, though? Offering a room in their home? Providing a hot shower and an amazing meal? That's too much. Too good to be true.

What if he's working for my uncle?

Fear spikes through my veins, causing me to jump off the bed. I stand, frozen in place, listening to everything around me. My skin prickles with awareness as I catalog every sound, from the clock ticking to the dishwasher running downstairs.

Could the kind, understanding man from the coffee shop be fooling me? Could he be trying to make me comfortable enough to let my guard down, only to toss me in the back of his car and drop me off with my uncle?

But he's already had the opportunity if that's what he wanted. I fell asleep on the ride to Armando's house, so wouldn't it have made more sense to get rid of me then?

My head spins with possibilities and doubts. There's one sure way to know if I can trust Armando.

I slowly make my way to the door, resting my hand on

the knob. I remember Armando telling me I could lock him out. In my experience, doors lock from the *outside*, keeping whoever is inside trapped. Namely, me. Is this just another cage I've walked into?

Taking a deep breath, I turn the knob, pushing the door open to reveal an empty hallway. Huh. I guess that's one point in Armando's favor.

I peek out, looking left and right, but no one is in sight. Shoring up what little courage I have, I step into the hallway and head for the warm light coming from downstairs.

I'm unsure what I expected to find, but it certainly wasn't Armando reclining on the couch with a book. He looks uncomfortable with his foot tapping up and down and his shoulders hunched up to his ears. As I reach the bottom of the stairs, I see he's holding the book upside down.

Weird.

Armando peers over the top of the book, and his eyes meet mine. A smile takes over his features, and his shoulders drop as if all his tension drains away when he sees me. He's genuinely excited and relieved, and I blink back tears. I don't think anyone has ever been this happy to see me. The doubts from earlier vanish the longer I look at him.

"Hey, sweetheart," Armando greets me, his smile growing bigger as I clear the last stair and walk into the living room. Hazel eyes catch mine, and the emotion there is overwhelming and unfamiliar.

"Good book?" I ask, eyeing the well-worn paperback.

Armando flips through the pages and then realizes it's upside down. The tips of his ears turn red, and oh my god, is he blushing? How is it possible for the hulking giant of a man to be this adorable?

"You caught me," he says sheepishly, closing the book and setting it on the coffee table. "I was worried about you and couldn't figure out what to do with myself. After nearly wearing a hole in my hardwood floors from pacing, I thought I'd try to get some reading in." Armando rubs the back of his neck and looks at the book before returning his magical eyes to mine. "As you can see, it didn't go very well."

He was worried about me? My heart flips in my chest, but I try not to let it mean anything. He's being nice for reasons I still can't comprehend.

I'm drawn to Armando, my feet padding forward without my permission. I can't explain it, but I need to be near him. I need his calming touch, grounding scent, and deep, comforting voice that sends tingles racing up and down my spine.

"Can I get you anything?" he asks. "Water? Food?"

"Oh, that's okay. I ate before my nap."

"I'm guessing that was shortly after I left for work?"

I nod and look out the front window, noticing for the first time that it's dark out.

"I figured. That was nearly seven hours ago."

My eyes widen when I realize how long I've slept. "Sorry, I'm a terrible guest," I mumble, automatically wrapping my arms around my middle for protection.

"Allegra," Armando whispers, standing in front of me. "No more apologies, remember?" He crooks his pointer finger and tips my chin so we're eye to eye. "You needed sleep, and I'm happy I could provide that for you. I was concerned you were sick."

I shake my head and am immediately rewarded with a dazzling grin. Good lord, this man is devastating in the best possible way. I could get addicted to a smile like that.

"I'm feeling a lot better than this morning," I tell him truthfully. "Thank you. For everything. I don't know what I would've done if…" I trail off, not wanting to think about it.

"Good thing we don't have to worry about that," Armando says softly. "I'm here, and you're safe."

"Safe," I repeat in a whisper. He keeps telling me that, like he knows I don't believe it yet.

"That's right, Allegra." Armando cups the side of my face, holding me still as he leans down and presses the lightest kiss to my forehead. He immediately drops his hand and steps back, leaving me cold and swaying on my feet. "I'm sorry, that was too much," he rushes to say, taking another step back.

I grab his hand and keep him anchored to me, pulling his muscled frame closer. "Not too much," I murmur. "I… I like being near you," I admit.

A second later, his arms are around me. "Good," he grunts, pressing our bodies together. "I like it, too."

After a few moments of being engulfed in Armando's embrace, he loosens his grip and guides us to sit on the couch. I try sitting next to him, but Armando isn't having any of that. His hands slide down my waist until he's circling my hips and pulling me down on his lap.

"Still okay?" he asks, his lips brushing the shell of my ear.

I nod, leaning against his solid chest. Armando hums in approval, and the vibrations of his voice echo through my veins until they reach my throbbing core.

It's inappropriate, and I have zero experience in this department, but tell that to the ache blooming between my thighs. I wiggle a bit to get comfortable, and Armando groans. His fingers dig into my hips, creating a sense of urgency.

"Careful, angel. You have no idea what you do to me. I'm trying to be a good man when it comes to you."

"You are a good man," I tell him firmly, looking at him over my shoulder. "You've done more for me in the short time I've known you than anyone in my family…"

My voice cracks, and I close my eyes, curling in on myself at the thought of my family.

"You don't have to tell me everything," Armando whispers. "But I need to ask some questions, okay? I need to know how I can keep you safe."

I freeze, not wanting to relive everything that brought me to this point. Armando leans back on the couch and readjusts my position so I'm sitting sideways on his lap. On instinct, I relax against his chest and tuck my head into his neck. My gentle giant cradles me in his arms, combing his fingers through my hair.

"I know, sweet girl," he coos. "I know it hurts. Do you trust me?"

"Yes," I whisper into his skin.

"Let me in. Just a little, Allegra. I promise to protect all the pieces of your heart."

"You don't even know me," I remind him. My voice is so quiet I don't know if he heard me.

"That's not true," he counters, his tone matching mine. "I know you're brave as hell to get out of whatever situation you were in. And we've established how strong and selfless you are. We've also been over how beautiful you are, inside and out."

God, his words pour over me like a calming salve to my broken, battered heart.

"Okay," I finally murmur, nodding once. "I'll answer some questions."

"Good girl," he rasps, pressing his lips to my temple.

My skin sizzles whenever he calls me that, but I try pushing those thoughts aside and focusing on the questions.

"You told me earlier you were running from a bad man."

I nod, bracing myself for the next part.

"Who hurt you, Allegra? Who was chasing you?"

"My uncle," I whisper.

"Was he the one who left bruises on your skin?"

I nod, folding in on myself to be as small as possible.

"Jesus," he grunts. "And he's still looking for you?"

"He'll never stop," I admit, my voice barely more than a whimper.

"I've got you," Armando reminds me, smoothing his hand up and down my back while holding me close. "He'll never hurt you again, angel. I promise."

We sit in silence for a few moments while Armando absorbs the little information I've given him. Eventually, he peels me off his chest so we're face to face.

"Can you tell me what happened this morning? What sent you running?"

I take a deep breath and look up at the ceiling, willing the tears to recede until later when I'm alone in bed. Armando has already wiped away too many of my tears to count.

"He was always angry," I whisper, still unable to look Armando in the eye. "He became my guardian when I was eleven. I never knew my dad, and my mom struggled with numerous addictions until she finally succumbed to an overdose. I almost ended up in a group home, but a lawyer found a will my mom drew up after I was born and named my uncle, Tommy, my legal guardian. He's hated me ever since."

"I'm so sorry," Armando says, his breath tickling my lips. "Was it your uncle who gave you that scar, sweetheart?"

The question surprises me, but what shocks me more is that I want to tell him. I finally look into Armando's multi-colored eyes, finding deep sympathy and understanding in their depths. It gives me the courage to continue.

"We had a fight," I whisper, swallowing down the emotion clogging my throat. "I was thirteen, and he forgot to pick me up from middle school. I walked home and interrupted him with a woman, and… it wasn't pretty. She left, which sent my uncle into a rage. He pulled a knife on me, and I thought… I thought he was going to kill me," I say in a rush before my voice cracks.

"Jesus Christ," Armando growls, tension coursing through his muscles.

"I got out of his hold and ran to my room, where I shoved my dresser and anything I could find in front of my door. My uncle never tried to open it. He didn't say anything the next day, even when I had a huge bandage on. When he got home from work that night, he tossed me a bottle of super glue and said, *go patch yourself up.*"

"Allegra, fuck," he mutters in disbelief. The tips of his fingers find my scar, stroking the raised skin. Instead of feeling ashamed, I feel seen and understood.

"Things got better for a while when I started waitressing at his… business establishment." I stumble over the last two words, not wanting to admit what it was. A sketchy strip club offering anything for those willing to pay the right price. "I thought maybe we had turned a new leaf, and he needed proof I wasn't going to mooch off him forever. I wanted to show him I could earn my keep, you know?"

"You shouldn't have had to prove yourself, sweet girl. It was his responsibility to care for you."

I shrug, dismissing his words. The concept of getting something for nothing is absurd, but I don't tell him that. I have a feeling Armando is going to prove me wrong.

"After I graduated high school, I worked more hours, but it wasn't enough to pay the rent he started charging me. I ended up staying at… Well, it doesn't matter. I survived. I was working on saving up and getting out of here for good, but then…"

I break eye contact as every muscle in my body tenses. I can still feel his hand wrapped around my bicep, his fingers digging into my skin as he dragged me out of my makeshift bed in the closet. I can still smell his alcohol-soaked breath as he told me I had been promoted to serve exclusively in the VIP lounge.

"Breathe for me, baby," Armando murmurs, cupping my cheek and tilting my head. I do as he says, inhaling deeply and exhaling, my eyes never leaving his. "Good girl."

I sit up a little straighter, loving his praise even in the midst of telling him my whole fucked up situation. "This morning, my uncle informed me I would be working in the VIP lounge," I continue, my voice shaky but still there. "It's, um, a lounge for... uh, men who have lots of money and want to spend it on treating women like objects."

"Goddammit," Armando growls, his features turning hard as stone while he listens. "Did anyone touch you? Like that? Fuck, angel, please tell me they didn't..."

"No," I rush to say. "I refused. I fought him off. I knew I wouldn't survive if I went through something like that. I somehow got out of his hold and bolted outside. I had no idea where to go or what to do. I just had to keep going, putting one foot in front of the other until... until..."

"Until you found your safe space," Armando finishes. "Until you found me."

I nod, resting my forehead on his. "Until I found you," I repeat softly.

We breathe together, our hearts beating in sync as Armando rubs his nose against mine. It's such a sweet, tender moment, and I can't believe I met this man less than twenty-four hours ago. Still, our connection is undeniable.

"Are you going to kiss me?" I whisper, my cheeks immediately burning with the boldness of my question.

Armando groans, rolling his forehead against mine. "I want to, angel. But you understand why I can't, right? It would kill me if you ever thought I was taking advantage of you, of your vulnerability. You came to me for help."

"I came to you for safety," I correct, staring at his lips. "And you make me feel safe enough to do anything. Safe enough to sleep, safe enough to tell my story, safe enough to ask for what I want."

The hulking man trembles beneath me, his muscles shaking with the effort of holding back. Knowing how much I affect him sends a delicious shiver down my spine.

"What do you want, sweet girl? I'll give you anything." God, his voice is deep and filled with dark desire that slices through my nerves and spikes my awareness.

"I want you to be my first kiss," I whisper.

"Your first..." Armando inhales sharply, his nostrils flaring as his hazel eyes turn dark brown. "I'm going to hell for wanting you the way I do, but Jesus, I can't stop."

His mouth is on mine in the next second, nipping at my lips until I open up for him. I moan as his tongue slides against mine, lapping at me in steady strokes. He tangles his fingers in my hair, angling my head so he can dive deeper and give me everything I've been missing.

I fist his shirt and claw at his chest, grinding on his lap with each toe-curling stroke of his tongue. Armando growls into our kiss, skimming his other hand down my back to grab my ass in a punishing hold. He holds me in place while rubbing his thick erection into my core, causing me to cry out when he hits some super sensitive spot.

"Allegra," he rasps, finally breaking the kiss. We're both gasping for breath, the frantic need for each other hanging in the air. "So sweet. So responsive for me."

He nuzzles into the side of my neck as his arms circle my back, pulling me in for a hug. It's surprisingly tender after the way we just devoured each other, but I need this, too. Need his gentle care after such a mind-blowing first kiss.

I'm not sure how much time has passed when I'm jostled awake. I don't remember falling asleep.

"I've got you," Armando whispers, carrying me through the house. "I'll tuck you into bed, angel. We'll deal with everything else tomorrow."

I nod, snuggling into his chest. It's the safest, most loved I've ever felt.

CHAPTER FIVE

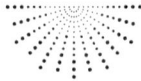

ARMANDO

"*How* ow is Cambria adjusting to life in New York? And your father?" Romeo asks Dante.

The inner circle members are all in Romeo's office for our weekly update and assignments.

"Just fine," Dante answers in a clipped tone. He's not nearly as aloof as he once was, though he would claim otherwise. Still, his voice has more warmth than usual, and I know it's all thanks to his new woman, Cambria.

"And the dumb fucks who kidnaped them have been dealt with, correct?"

"Affirmative," Dante growls. "I took out the leader of their little group of rebels, and the Moscatellis took care of the rest. They didn't appreciate another family on their territory, and they promised to contact me if they found any more Colombos in Chicago."

"They're good allies to have," Romeo says, pacing his office. Whenever the Boss is fidgeting instead of sitting at his desk and brooding, I know it's going to be a busy week. "While the Moscatellis keep tabs on our enemies in Chicago, we'll do the same here. After their attempt to harm my Thalia and the lives we took to get her back, I know they'll retaliate. I can't say for sure how the Colombos feel about the group of thugs who came for Cambria without permission, but we can't rule out their wrath for that incident, either. This game is about pride, and we've damaged theirs."

"What do we need to do, Boss?" I ask.

My foot won't stop tapping up and down, and I know I sound more than a little eager to get going. It's not out of character for me to be impatient while awaiting instructions, but today I'm antsier than usual. I have a beautiful warrior goddess in my home, waiting for me to return. Fuck yeah, I'm itching to get back to her.

"We'll focus on gathering information from our mutual connections. Dante, you and I will invite some of the financial world's bigger players to a black-tie dinner to get a read on where Colombo money is going."

Dante nods, scribbling down notes. What a nerd.

"My specialty isn't tuxedos and champagne, it's back-alley brawling," I mutter under my breath.

Romeo spins on his heel and narrows his eyes at me. "I'm used to you wanting to get out there and crack skulls, but you seem particularly restless today, Armando," he says carefully, assessing every one of my breaths. He's trying to get a read on me, but I don't mind.

"I am, but I'm always ready to give two hundred percent. You know that," I respond.

After a beat of silence, Romeo nods once before continuing. "You and Valentino will handle our contacts on the ground. Known business fronts, strip clubs, the seedier side of our city. They'll likely talk more than the financial hotshots, but their intel can't always be trusted. I know both of you will use your best judgment on what information makes it back inside this office."

Valentino and I share a look, then nod in deference to the Don.

"Yes, Boss," Valentino answers.

"Of course, Boss," I add.

"Good. It's settled. This is our number one priority. We need to strike while they're still scrambling."

Romeo dismisses us a few minutes later, and Valentino follows me into the hallway.

"You, uh, doing okay?" he asks, giving me some side-eye. "You seem ready to bolt out of here. Don't tell me you have some chick waiting for you."

"She's not *some chick*," I snarl, looking Valentino dead in the eye.

Valentino is the youngest member of the Di Salvo family inner circle, but he's proven himself loyal in a short amount of time. Valentino's past is a bit of a mystery, and while Dante has his suspicions, I know better than to question the Boss's decisions. If Romeo says he's legit, then he's legit.

Right now, however, I want to rearrange his face with my fist for disrespecting Allegra.

"Jesus, not you, too," he groans. "First Romeo, then Dante, and now…" Valentino sighs as he gestures vaguely in my direction.

"You have an opinion about the Boss' woman? I'm sure he'd love to hear it."

The tall, tatted-up man raises his palms in mock surrender. "Not trying to start anything. Just saying I don't understand. You all went so long without having these… entanglements, so why start now?"

"First, I'm only eight years older than you. Don't talk to me like I'm elderly," I grunt. "And second, by *entanglements,* you mean…?"

Valentino rolls his eyes, exasperated by my question. "I mean all the complications that come with women and relationships in general. All three of you are at the top of your game, so I don't understand why you're so willing to throw it all away."

"Who says Romeo is throwing anything away? Is he not still the Boss? And is Dante not still his second in command? Why would being in a relationship change that?"

"Hey man, I'm just calling it like I see it. The more attachments a person has, the more there is to lose. I just figured men like us, having the careers we have, would think twice about falling in love."

It's true that Valentino is only eight years younger than my thirty-nine, but right now, he looks like a petulant child with his nose scrunched up. This tempers some of my initial anger. Valentino isn't being an ass; he just has a giant chip on his shoulder. Interesting.

"When it happens to you, you'll understand there's no choice," I tell him, resuming my walk out of the house and over to my parked car. I have a driver for almost everything except for my meetings at the compound.

"When what happens to me?" Valentino asks, trailing along behind me.

"When you fall in love. It's not really falling, in my experience," I muse, remembering the moment I saw Allegra. "It's more like getting clobbered."

Valentino snorts. "And you're advocating this? Getting clobbered by love?"

I unlock my car and slip inside the driver's seat, looking up at my colleague through the open car door. "It's the best goddamn thing that's ever happened to me."

"You're crazy," he scoffs, though I see the hint of a smile.

"A piece of advice, kid?" I say with a smirk. "When it happens to you, don't fight it. You won't win."

"Whatever," Valentino mutters as I close the car door. "I'll call you tomorrow morning, and we'll plan our week," he shouts as I rev the engine.

I nod once, then peel out of the Di Salvo compound with one thought on my mind. *Allegra.*

The normally twenty-minute drive home takes only ten. I try taking a few deep breaths to calm myself, but my heart won't stop racing. I've only been away for three hours, but I miss my angel already.

When I step inside, I'm greeted with the sweetest sight; my Allegra in an oversized t-shirt, humming to herself while wiping down the kitchen counter. Her hips sway to the tune in her head, and the sunlight pouring in through the window catches on her strawberry-blonde hair, making it glitter.

My feet carry me forward as if in a trance, my eyes unable to part from her for a single second. Allegra looks up at me, and her blue eyes light up when they meet mine. God, she's perfection. Sweet, innocent, tempting perfection.

"Welcome home," she says seconds before I scoop her up in my arms.

"Love seeing you in my clothes," I grunt like an animal.

Allegra giggles and I have to capture the sound on my tongue. Our lips meet softly at first and then with more passion. I open my mouth, needing more, needing to consume her and tie her to me in every way. Our tongues tangle, each giving and taking in perfect measure.

Never breaking our kiss, I walk Allegra backward and set her on the counter before stepping between her parted thighs. My girl moans for me, her aching core rubbing against the thick, painful erection trapped in my pants.

I need more. I need her skin under my tongue, need to lap at those perky nipples, need to breathe her in. I need to see her come. I need to smell her release as it drips down my chin.

Reluctantly, I break our kiss so I can fill my lungs with

air. She follows me like our lips are connected by magnets. It pleases me to know she's as addicted to me as I already am to her.

I watch as she catches her breath, her eyes closed, her lips swollen, and her cheeks flushed.

"Beautiful," I whisper into the side of her neck before placing a soft kiss there.

Allegra's pulse beats rapidly, making me groan and lick the same spot. She bucks her hips, grazing her hot little pussy against me.

"Do you like when I kiss you here, Allegra?" I ask as I continue trailing kisses up and down her slender column.

"Yes, sir," she whimpers.

I growl into her skin, my already hard dick turning to granite at her words. Goddamn, I didn't know what a turn-on that would be, but I can't get enough. She arches her neck, baring the soft flesh to me. I'm like a wolf, ready to sink my teeth into my prey.

"Fucking love when you call me that," I growl again, sucking and licking and nipping as she moans for me.

My lips trail lower, grazing her collarbone, where I suck and bite her, just enough to turn her skin pink, not enough to leave a mark. But fuck, I want to mark her. Claim her. Devour her.

"Please," Allegra whimpers as I slowly kiss my way down her chest and over the fabric of her shirt. "I need more. Please, Armando."

"Who?" I ask before rolling her nipple in between my lips.

"Sir! Please, sir…"

I reward her by slipping my fingers under her shirt to explore her silky-smooth skin. My large, rough hands skim her soft tummy, higher, higher, until my thumbs graze the sensitive underside of her breasts.

Allegra lifts her arms, giving me permission to explore

more of her luscious body. I grip the hem of the too-large shirt and slowly slide it up her body, revealing inch after creamy inch of skin to my hungry eyes.

I practically tear the shirt off her, then stand back to admire the most perfect pair of tits I've ever seen.

"Fucking hell," I whisper. I brush the back of my knuckles down the top of one breast and over the pebbled nipple, loving how she trembles at my touch.

Leaning down, I lick over her aching peaks before blowing cold air on them. Allegra gasps, and her thighs tighten around my waist. I suck on her breast *hard*, loving how her body fits perfectly with mine. I caress her thick thighs as I suck and nibble one breast and then the other. She leans back with her hands on the counter, thrusting her chest out for me and pushing her breast deeper into my mouth.

I groan at her offering and pop off her tit, only to repeat the process on the other one. The whole time, my thumbs massage circles on the insides of Allegra's thighs, inching higher and higher.

"Oh, God, ohmygod, I..."

Allegra trembles beneath my touch, and I swear she's going to come from this alone. She cries out as I pull her nipple through my teeth, her legs shaking, her heart pounding in her chest. I feel the heat of her pussy as she grinds down against my throbbing cock, seeking the friction she needs.

"I'm... I think..."

My hands slide around her back, holding her up as her arms give out. Allegra throws her head back in a silent scream as I bite her nipple. I watch in complete awe as this goddess falls apart in my arms. I feel every muscle in her back tense and release as I hold her close and kiss all over her breasts and neck.

Finally, Allegra goes limp in my arms. I gather her up and hold her close to my chest, kissing the top of her head.

"So sensitive," I murmur as I stroke her back. "So damn responsive."

She looks up at me and blushes, burying her head in my chest again. "Sorry," she whispers. "Is that bad?"

"Not at all. I love it. I love that I get to explore your body and show you how good you can feel."

She tries hiding from me, but I peel away one small hand and then the other, placing a kiss on both palms and wrapping them around my neck.

I rest my forehead on hers and breathe her in. "Do you trust me, sweetheart?"

"Yes, sir," she whispers.

I grunt in approval and kiss my way down her neck and chest until I'm nuzzling between her perfect mounds.

And then I kiss lower.

My lips trail over her ribcage and stomach as I gently lay her out on the counter and kneel in front of her.

"Am I going to be the first to lick your dripping pussy? The first to taste you and suck on your needy little clit?"

Allegra moans as I hook my thumbs in the waistband of the boxers she's wearing. I pause until I hear her say it.

"Yes, sir, only you."

I slide the boxers off her and trail kisses up the inside of one thigh and then the other. I stroke my fingers through the soft patch of curls decorating her mound and grin when she shivers and squirms.

"And will I be the first to dip my fingers into your tight little cunt?"

"Yes!"

I smack her pussy, not too hard, and Allegra spasms and gasps in surprise.

"Yes, who?"

41

She's panting now, her fingers gripping the side of the counter so hard her knuckles are white. "Yes, sir. Please," she whimpers.

"Love when you beg so nicely for me, angel," I growl as I throw her legs over my shoulders.

I part her lips with my thumbs and stare at the most decadent pussy I've ever seen. She's soaking wet, and her clit is engorged and throbbing for me. Precum leaks from my aching cock as her scent washes over me.

Her body shakes in my hands, vibrating with need and anticipation. I blow warm air over her tight cunt, watching it convulse as a wave of wetness gushes from her virgin hole. One drop of honey trickles down to her puckered little asshole, and I lick it up, not stopping until I circle her clit with the tip of my tongue.

"Armando…" Her voice cracks as she gasps for air.

God, her sounds… Fuck, it makes my cock throb and my balls ache. How can she unravel me with just that small thing?

"Say it again," I demand.

"Armando," she moans. "I like how it feels."

"Good," I murmur. "I like the way it makes you say my name."

I lap at her sweet pussy, spearing my tongue inside her entrance and scooping up more of her juices to swirl around her clit. Allegra's hips buck against me, her thighs tighten around my head, and I can tell she's about to let go for me.

But I want to drag it out.

I look up from between her legs and watch her tits rise and fall as she pants for air. Everything about her is captivating.

I slowly lick the seam where her leg meets her hip, first one and then the other. I trace the outside of her pussy lips and dart my tongue into her slit, licking her clit once. She twists, and I move my tongue back to lazy circles around her folds and dips. I repeat this process, torturing her, bringing her closer and closer, one lick at a time.

Sucking her clit into my mouth, I swipe my tongue over the tight bundle of nerves again and again until her muscles pull tight and her breath catches in her throat. And then…

I back away, grinning when I hear her frustrated grunt.

"I need more," she whines, twisting beneath me.

"Trust me, Allegra. I'll make it worth the wait."

I play with my girl some more, swiping a finger up and down her pussy, chuckling when her greedy cunt tries to suck me inside.

"So damn sexy," I tell her before plunging my finger inside her.

"Oh!" Her surprised little yelp turns into a moan as I pump in and out. "More!"

I withdraw my finger and smack her clit, making her gush for me and cry out. I plunge two fingers into her tight channel, in and out, curling them up and rubbing them over her G-spot. I take them out just as quickly and smack her pussy again.

"How do good girls ask for what they want?"

"More, sir, please, please…"

I growl in approval and shove three fingers inside her dripping pussy while biting down on her clit. Allegra bows her back off the kitchen counter, every muscle in her body drawn up tight. Then she jerks her hips up and thrashes underneath me so hard I have to keep my other hand over her stomach to keep her from falling off the damn counter.

I keep fingerfucking her as her pussy squeezes me tightly, my thumb taking the place of my mouth so I can watch her curvy body get overtaken by pleasure. When Allegra gasps for air, I can tell she thinks it's over.

But I keep going. I curl my fingers up again while keeping

her pinned to the counter. I feel it. I *feel* her orgasm deep in her core, rising to the surface as I beckon it with my fingers deep inside her.

"Armando, I'm…"

"Let it happen, Allegra. Let go for me."

"Ah, ah, ah, oh fuck, ohmygod, there, right there…"

Allegra screams and shatters so beautifully for me. I withdraw my hand and bury my face between her legs, gripping her ass and bringing her closer to me so I can drink her release. I can't breathe, but I don't give a fuck. She's exquisite.

"Too… much…" She tries to twist out of my grip.

I snarl like the feral beast she makes me, licking her pussy clean until the final tremors of her orgasm leave her in a shuddering breath.

I stand, scooping Allegra's limp body into my arms and sitting us on the couch, with her curled up in my lap. It's a special kind of hell having the sexiest woman I've ever seen naked on my lap. My cock aches and is harder than it's ever been, but this wasn't about me. Her pleasure will always come first.

I cup her head with one hand and tuck her into my chest, stroking her bare back with my other hand, hoping to comfort her after such an intense first sexual experience.

"You did so good. You're so brave, letting me have control of your pleasure like that," I whisper before kissing the top of her head. "Are you okay, sweetheart?"

Allegra takes a stuttering breath, and for a moment, I worry I've pushed her too far.

"I've never felt… I didn't know…" She sighs. "I'm so good, Armando. I mean, sir."

I chuckle and kiss the top of her head again. "You can call me Armando. Sir is for when we play. Do you understand?"

She nods into my chest.

"Need your words, Allegra."

"I understand."

"Good girl. My sweet angel," I praise. "Rest now. I'll be here when you wake up."

No sooner do the words leave my mouth than her eyes flutter closed. I grab a blanket from the back of the couch and drape it over her gorgeous body, needing her to be safe and warm above all else.

CHAPTER SIX

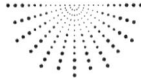

ALLEGRA

*S*omething tickles my chin, then my cheek, slowly moving up, up, up, until I feel the soft tickling on my temple. Slowly blinking one eye open, I'm greeted with hazel eyes and a warm smile.

"There you are," Armando whispers, nuzzling his nose against mine.

"Here I am," I answer sleepily as a yawn escapes. The more I wake up, the more aware I am of my surroundings. Armando is holding me on his lap on the couch, and from the looks of the orange sunlight streaming through the front window, we've been here for a while. "Sorr–"

Armando cuts me off with a quick kiss. "I hope you weren't about to apologize." He lifts a skeptical eyebrow.

"Who, me? I would *never!*" I bat my eyelashes dramatically, making him grin.

"Love seeing your sassy side," he murmurs before kissing me again, for real this time.

Armando slides his tongue against mine, striking a match with each stroke until my body is on fire for him. One of his hands sneaks under the blanket I'm wrapped up in, his rough fingertips tickling my sensitive flesh. My arms circle his neck as I cling to him, my need growing more urgent with each passing second.

"Gotta stop," he grits, breaking our kiss to trail his lips down my neck. "I don't want to pressure you or make you uncomfortable."

"I'm comfortable," I breathe, leaning forward and stealing a kiss. "I could be more comfortable, though," I pant. The blanket falls from my body, leaving me naked in his arms. Rolling my hips forward, I gasp when I feel his thick dick harden even more beneath me.

"Jesus, Allegra. Need you to tell me exactly what you mean." Armando grips my hips, holding me in place while grinding against my soaking-wet center. "Fuck me, angel. I'm trying to be good…"

"Be bad with me," I whisper, brushing my lips over the shell of his ear.

Who is this bold woman speaking through me right now?

I don't have time to question my newfound sense of confidence. Not when Armando is looking at me like I hold his life in my hands. A pained sound rumbles up from his chest as his hips jerk, grinding his massive cock against my swollen pussy.

"Please, sir," I moan, loving how it's working him up. "Please… *fuck* me."

Armando lets out a savage snarl as he leaps to his feet, tossing me over his shoulder as he bounds up the stairs.

"Hey!" I shout, though I'm mostly laughing.

My man palms my ass, giving it a squeeze before smacking it. "You're killing me," he groans. "This sexy fucking body…"

The next thing I know, I'm falling through the air before my back hits the soft mattress. Armando falls on top of me, pinning me down with his weight, blanketing me in his strength. His lips are on mine, picking up where we left off in the living room.

Armando holds himself up with one hand at the side of my head while his other slides down my body, cupping my breast. He squeezes lightly, groaning into my mouth. Then his hand moves lower, gripping my hip, sliding down my thigh, and tickling my bare skin. He squeezes me there and groans again, pulling my leg to the side so he can settle between my thighs.

"Need to get naked, but I can't stop kissing these lips," he whispers, grinding himself against my core as he kisses me again.

I make some desperate sound in the back of my throat, then tear my mouth from his, breathing fresh air into my burning lungs. Armando rests his forehead on mine, taking deep, ragged breaths. Knowing he's this wound up because of me is even more of a confidence booster.

I push on his chest, giving him a devious grin as he sits up. I follow him, standing right in front of the ripped demigod of a man. I tug at his shirt, silently demanding that he take it off. His eyes flash with wicked intentions that match mine as he pulls his shirt off.

My hands find his chest, my fingers teasing his skin in featherlight touches. Lower, lower, lower my exploration goes, learning the dips in his defined chest and abs. A shiver runs through his body and into mine, drawing us closer together.

I still can't believe he wants me. I'm a mess, inside and out. My life is falling apart, and I have zero experience. Not to mention, Armando is like a twenty on a scale of one to ten, and I'm hovering at about a three. In no world does this strong, sexy, surprisingly sweet man choose me.

Armando tips my chin and kisses me soundly as his fingers tangle in my hair and tug at the strands. I let go of every thought, moaning softly when his other hand slides up my spine, caressing my skin in barely there touches, despite his obvious need for me.

I'm so lost in his touch, it takes me a second to realize he's trailing kisses over the ugly scar on my neck. Instinctively, I pull back, turning my head to hide the mark.

"Allegra," he says softly. "What did I tell you about your scars?"

"They prove I'm a survivor," I whisper, my eyes locking onto his.

"Good girl. That's right. Every part of you is perfect. Every inch. Can I show you?"

Armando doesn't push me for an answer, he simply offers me his hand. *How does he know exactly what I need?*

I slip my hand in his, letting him pull me closer as his eyes roam up and down my chest, torso, and legs before reversing their path. When Armando finally meets my gaze again, he gives me a gentle, reverent look. He's letting me know he wants to cherish me as much as he wants to devour me. I feel the same.

"You're so beautiful, angel," he murmurs. "I'm going to ravish every inch of you, Allegra. I hope you're ready for that."

My core clenches and releases, making more of my arousal drip down my thighs. I can't keep my eyes off his hands, which are working furiously to rid himself of his clothing. As soon as he's naked in all of his glory, he grips my hips and walks me backward until my knees hit the edge of the mattress.

Armando cups my face in his hands and brushes his nose up and down mine in the lightest touch. "Do you trust me?"

"Yes, sir. With all of me," I don't hesitate to answer.

We share a tender moment, so many unspoken words passed back and forth with just one look. Then his hard length grazes against my center, and just like that, I'm aching for his touch.

Armando tips his head back and groans when I grab his cock and rub the tip with my thumb, spreading his precum around. "Fuck, you feel so good. I'm clean, Allegra. I haven't been with anyone in years. A decade or more. I want inside your tight, wet heat with nothing between us, but I'll put a condom on if you want."

"I want to feel you, too," I whisper, my cheeks heating at my words. I should feel embarrassed, but there's no room for shame when Armando is looking at me like that. He wants me as much as I want him, and I'm not about to ruin this moment for anything.

"Goddamn," he growls, pushing me down on the bed.

I'm expecting him to join me, but he sinks to his knees instead. He grips my thighs in his large hands and pries my legs apart. I cry out and bow my back off the bed when he presses his thumb over my clit. A sudden powerful burst of pleasure slices through me and rattles me to my core.

My pleasure grows more intense when his tongue slides through my dripping folds, licking me and nipping at my sensitive flesh. He nudges my clit with his nose and spears his tongue into my little hole, scooping out my juices and drinking them.

Armando drags his tongue lower, lower, lower, until it's teasing my back entrance. I gasp at the filthiness of it all, but the forbidden nature makes me even wetter. He licks around the tight ring of muscle and growls.

"Oh god," I whisper. "Ohmygod, Armando, oh fuck." My whisper becomes a loud moan when the very tip of his tongue pushes inside. He rubs my clit in furious circles, and I grip the sheets, twisting them in my fists as my body expands and contracts. "I'm…"

I shatter before I even finish my sentence. My orgasm

rushes through me with such intensity, I shoot up off the bed, trying to escape the overwhelming pleasure. Armando shoves me back down with a hand spread over my stomach. He holds me there, making me feel all of it, every last drop of bliss.

He grunts in satisfaction, crawling up my body and crashing his mouth down on mine in a passionate kiss. "Needed your taste on my tongue before I fuck this tight little pussy for the first time."

Leaning back slightly, Armando gathers my hands and guides them over my head. Pinning my wrists down, he drags his thickness through my folds, coating himself in my cream before lining up with my entrance.

"Ready, Allegra?"

"Yes. God. Yes, sir," I breathe.

He kisses me as he thrusts all the way inside, tearing through the last barrier between us. I tense up at the slight pinch deep in my core, holding my breath until it passes.

"I'm sorry," he whispers. "It won't hurt after this. I'll make you feel so good, angel. So fucking good."

"I'm okay," I promise him. "I want you so bad. Please don't stop."

"I'll take care of you, Allegra. My good girl. Always."

I nod and clench around his hard length, making him groan. I'm so full, stretched to the point of pain, but in the best way possible. It heightens my pleasure, sparks my nerves, and makes me thrust my hips, taking him deeper.

"Then do it, already," I practically growl at him.

Armando chuckles, and I feel the vibrations with every inch of me, inside and out.

He leans down and kisses the side of my neck, biting down gently on my pulse point. I writhe beneath him, pleasure taking over the pain. Armando pulls out almost all the way, hovering above me and driving me crazy.

Armando gives me a dark, delicious look before thrusting back inside me. His thickness scrapes along my walls, the friction like striking a match as instant, overwhelming heat engulfs me. I bow my back and push against his hand still holding my wrists, grateful for an anchor in the raging storm of sensations.

He pulls my leg higher on his hip, changing the angle. I whimper as his cock slides against some magical place inside me that has me sobbing his name louder with each thrust. He snaps his hips, grinding his pelvis against my clit while hitting that spot over and over.

Armando grunts my name every time his balls slap my ass. I can feel him losing control, his strokes becoming deeper, harder, so damn rough. I love it. I convulse as he thrusts into me relentlessly. The exquisite pleasure bordering on pain builds and builds, higher and higher, one more, one more, again, again… until I break. Shards of pleasure cut and heal me as I cry out for him repeatedly.

My orgasm rips through me, holding my body hostage, forcing me to feel every wave of bliss until tears drip down my face and I'm a sweaty, soaking mess beneath him. Armando stays still, buried deep inside my spasming pussy.

When the last of my pleasure leaves me, Armando growls and slams into me, letting go of my wrists and sliding his hand down my body. He squeezes my breast, leaning down and bringing the nipple to his mouth and lavishing it with attention until I'm shaking beneath him.

"Oh, God, Armando," I choke out. I claw at his back as he rips me apart in the best way possible. Each gut-twisting stroke winds me up higher and higher until I'm right on the precipice, teetering on the edge.

His hips stutter as he loses his rhythm and starts rutting into me. His fingers dig into my hips as my nails bite into his skin, both of us clinging to this tension-filled pleasure. A shiver runs through me, followed by another and another, until I'm shaking violently.

We both cry out as his hot seed spills into me. Wave after wave of his cum splashes into my pulsing channel and then drips out, and still, there's more. My pussy snaps around him as I sob my climax.

I gasp for air as I float back down to earth, the oxygen burning my lungs yet somehow sending jolts of pleasure to my core. Armando buries his face in my neck, and I wrap my arms around his torso, keeping him on top of me while we catch our breath.

"You're perfect," he whispers. "You're all mine."

I nod and pull him closer until most of his weight is resting on top of me.

Armando understands my need better than I do. He surrounds me with his strength, blanketing me in his warmth. "I'm right here, Allegra. I've got you."

We stay attached as long as possible, but I start to shiver from the sweat drying on my body. Armando rolls over and drags me with him, tucking me into his side. My eyelids grow heavy, and my body melts into his. I'm vaguely aware of Armando pulling the covers over us, but I'm too tired, too worn out to look.

"Get some sleep, sweetheart. I'll be right here when you wake up."

I nod, feeling safe, warm, and completely satisfied. As I drift off to sleep, I swear I hear Armando say he loves me. I want to say it back, but sleep takes me before I get a chance.

CHAPTER SEVEN

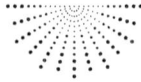

ARMANDO

I lie awake, listening to Allegra's soft snores and counting her breaths. I feel each intake of air as her lungs expand and contract. It's calming in a way I didn't know I needed.

The sun set quite a while ago, but my Allegra and I haven't moved. She passed out when I tucked her into my side, but I don't mind. The girl deserves to rest after what we did.

God, being with her was incredible. More than incredible. It was life-altering. Soul-shattering. Coming deep inside her was indescribable—the most profound moment of my life.

My dick grows hard thinking about her stretched out beneath me. She trusted me with her body, her virginity, and her pleasure. She begged me, and I'll never forget our first time together. I can't wait to be inside her again, but I know my girl has to be sore. Each thrust tore at my sanity until I lost my mind and fucked her so damn hard.

Allegra moans softly in her sleep, then wiggles her hips, trying to get closer to me. I can't stop the deep, hungry growl rising from my chest when she adjusts her leg and grazes my hard as fuck dick. She's still asleep, but her leg hooks around mine, her knee rubbing against my nearly painful erection.

I reach down and wrap my hand around the back of her knee. I mean to push her leg away so I don't come all over myself like a teenager, but instead, I find myself grinding against her. I sink my teeth into my bottom lip as unbelievable pleasure rolls through me. How can I be so close to the edge from just this simple touch?

But I already know the answer. It's her. Everything about her. I'll never get enough. I know I need to stop, but she feels so damn good. Precum leaks out of me, my raging hard-on needing some relief. When Allegra rubs her soaking wet core against my thigh, I groan loudly, unable to contain the sound.

Allegra returns my groan with one of her own, awareness slowly creeping into her movements as she wakes up. Her nails bite into my bare chest, snapping the last thread of my control. Wrapping her long hair around my fist, I tilt her head back, growling when I see her blue eyes ablaze. My lips are on hers in the next second.

I swallow down her cries of pleasure as I devour her. Her hot little body writhes against mine, creating delicious, torturous friction. I need more. Need to feel her from the inside out. Need to consume her, taste her sweat, bite her soft skin, and drink down everything she's offering.

"Armando," she whimpers into my mouth, capturing my lips again. I pull her on top of me so she's straddling my lap. Allegra breaks our kiss, gasping for air. "Armando," she repeats as she rolls her hips.

Allegra's pussy lips wrap around my cock, fluttering around my length and driving me insane. I've never had this overwhelmingly primal need to claim, to possess, to own someone completely. Allegra rests her forehead on mine as a shudder ripples through her soft, curvy body. I know she's as desperate as I am when a pained whimper escapes her mouth.

She sits up, steadying herself with both hands on my chest. I grip her hips and lift her, positioning her dripping wet hole over the head of my cock. I hiss out a breath and squeeze my eyes shut, trying with everything in me not to come like this. Her cunt pulses, massaging my sensitive dick and making me buck my hips involuntarily and slide a few inches inside her.

"Are you sure, angel?" I grit.

Instead of answering, Allegra bites her bottom lip and nods, her big blue eyes telling me everything I need to know. Slowly, so slowly, she sinks down on my length, her pussy stretching obscenely wide around my cock.

I drag my eyes up her body, taking in her pale skin and strawberry-blonde hair. She's practically glowing in the moonlight streaming through the window. I watch in awe as the silver light kisses the side of her face, her breasts, and her thighs. My fingers skim over everywhere the light touches, needing to feel this goddess as she brings me unimaginable pleasure.

Allegra tilts her head back and claws my chest, gasping for air once she's fully seated. I grip her hips, anchoring her to me, keeping her right here. Her core ripples around my cock, making the fucker jerk and leak more precum inside her.

"You feel so good," I whisper, unable to find my voice as I get lost in how our bodies are connected on every level.

I help her find her rhythm, rolling her hips and grinding her down on my swollen dick. Each movement sends sharp pangs of ecstasy shooting through my veins. I know she feels it, too, with each breathy moan that falls from her lips.

Allegra's eyes snap open, locking on mine. I see the moment she recognizes her power. Her strength. Those blue eyes turn fierce, almost feral, as she lifts on her knees and drops down on me, her little hole swallowing my dick completely.

An animalistic growl rumbles through her, wracking her body as she fucks me furiously. Christ, it's all I can do to hold on. I want this for her, need this, need her to take control and understand that I'm hers. She owns me, body and soul.

I cup the back of her neck and pull her down for a kiss, tasting her sweetness as she brings us closer, closer, closer…

"Armando," she whispers. "Armando… Armando… please, sir…" Her whimpers turn into moans, louder, louder, until she's crying out my name, her voice broken as she comes around my cock. Goddamn, she comes with her whole body, every muscle tensing and releasing as her orgasm works its way through her.

I keep her right here with me, her forehead resting on mine as she shakes and releases more of her juices. Her cum drips down my dick and coats my balls… and holy hell, is she coming again? Allegra buries her face in the side of my neck, muffling her scream as an intense orgasm rips through her curvy little body.

Something breaks loose inside me, leaving me unhinged and wild with need. I flip Allegra onto her back and rut into her throbbing pussy, grunting with each thrust. She bows her back and wraps her legs around my hips, digging her heels into my ass.

"That's it," I growl. "Such a good girl for me."

I lean down and suck on her breast, teasing one nipple and then the other, back and forth until her fingernails bite into the back of my head. She pulls my hair and tilts my head before slamming her mouth down on mine.

My greedy girl rocks into me, meeting me frantic thrust for frantic thrust. I break our kiss and inhale sharply as my orgasm barrels through me. With a roar, I let go of every fucking thing and come so damn hard my bones rattle.

Allegra's cries carve through the night air as her channel squeezes and snaps around me, milking me and prolonging our pleasure. We're both shaking and panting as we cling to each other, riding out the last of our climax.

I collapse on top of her, gathering her limp body in my arms. I try rolling to the side to keep from crushing her, but once again, Allegra urges me to stay right where I am. I'll be her safety blanket whenever she needs it. We stay wrapped up like that for long moments, Allegra taking deep breaths while I whisper how much she means to me and that she's safe in my arms.

Eventually, her grip on me loosens, allowing me to roll onto my back and drape her over my chest. After a few moments of silence, I begin to worry I've hurt her. I tore into her like a beast after taking her virginity only a few hours ago.

"Allegra?" I murmur, cupping the back of her neck and guiding her to look up at me. "Are you all right?" She nods, but I can't quite see the look on her face in the darkness of the room. "Need your words, angel. Did I… did I hurt you?"

"Not at all," she assures me.

The pressure in my chest releases, allowing me to breathe again.

"That was…" She nibbles her bottom lip, searching for something to describe what we just shared.

"Yeah, it was," I agree, kissing her forehead and the tip of her nose.

Allegra sighs contentedly before curling up on my chest again. We lie in silence for a few moments, soaking up the love we've found. It's on the tip of my tongue to tell her my intense feelings, but I'm not sure she's ready to hear it. Allegra has been through so much, and even though I'm ready for our forever, it's understandable for her to need more time.

I can be patient. I think. It's never been a particularly strong trait, but I'd do anything for my angel.

"This is seriously the comfiest bed in the world," Allegra sighs, snuggling up closer while pulling the blankets around her.

My chest grows tight at her words, remembering when she first stepped into her room and marveled at the sheets and pillows. I want to know everything about her, but I need to tread carefully.

I gently stroke Allegra's back, the tips of my fingers barely touching her silky-smooth skin as I trail them up and down her spine. She melts against me, letting me soothe every worry and doubt.

"Where were you sleeping before you met me?" I ask softly.

My sweet girl tenses and curls in on herself.

"Don't hide from me," I whisper, kissing the top of her head. "Remember who you are, Allegra. Strong, brave as fuck, kind, and beautiful. Nothing about your past can change that."

"How do you always know what to say?" she murmurs, tipping her head up. Blue eyes lock onto mine, and vulnerability clashes with growing confidence as she braces herself to tell me her truth.

"I'm not usually good with my words," I admit. "But with you… I'm trying so damn hard to be what you need."

"You are," Allegra whispers. She tucks her head into my neck, clinging to me while searching for her words. I'll wait however long she needs. "After my uncle kicked me out for being late on rent, I didn't know where to go. I still had my job as a waitress, and if I could find someplace to live for free, I'd be able to save enough money to get out and start over somewhere new."

I hum softly, resuming my steady, gentle strokes along her spine. I can tell Allegra has never spoken about this with anyone, and knowing she trusts me with her past and her secrets is humbling.

"Where did you end up?" I ask, though I'm sure I won't like the answer.

"I went into work like usual, then hid in the bathroom or out by the dumpsters until everyone else left around two-thirty or three in the morning. I sneaked back inside and made a little nest in a storage closet out of coats from the lost and found. Eventually, I stashed a blanket and pillow in the closet, but my uncle found them after a few weeks and threw them out after yelling at everyone for being lazy pieces of shit. I didn't try anything stupid like that again."

"Allegra," I murmur, cupping the back of her neck and nudging her to look up at me. "Jesus, sweetheart. I'm so sorry you had to live like that." She shrugs and looks away from me, but I don't let her get away with that. "I know what it's like to survive with nothing but the clothes on your back."

This gets her attention. Allegra gasps and her blue eyes grow wide. "What happened?"

"I…" Taking a breath, I let it out and focus on what's important. I can't derail this conversation with my sordid past, but I know we'll need to talk about everything soon. "This isn't about me right now, sweetheart. I need you to know I don't think less of you. It takes courage and persever-ance to push through that shit and wake up every morning. I'm so proud of you."

"Proud of… me?" Her voice is soft and broken, tugging at my heart painfully.

"Yes, sweet girl. You're a survivor."

"I don't deserve this," she whispers.

"Deserve what?"

"This… you, the bed, a fresh start. It's going to be ripped away. I'm going to screw it up, and–"

"Never," I say firmly, cutting her off as I flip her on her back and hover over her, caging in my beautiful angel with an arm on either side of her head. "You're not going to screw up anything, Allegra. Nothing is going to be ripped away. I'm your safe place, remember? And I'm not going anywhere."

My beautiful girl nods, cupping my cheek. I lean into her touch, closing my eyes and breathing in her sweet, honied scent. My lips are drawn to hers, and she opens up for me, accepting my kiss and asking for more.

"Thank you," she breathes against my lips before tangling her tongue with mine.

I groan as Allegra slides her hands into my hair, scratching my scalp and neck to pull me closer. I cover my sweet girl with my large frame, taking long, lazy sips from her addictive mouth.

"Never thank me," I rasp. "You give me everything just by breathing."

I rest my forehead on hers, sharing the same breath as we come back down. Rolling over on my back, I open my arms, smiling when Allegra snuggles into my side.

We still have a lot to talk about, including my career, but right now, I'm content to have the love of my life in my arms. We'll figure everything else out.

CHAPTER EIGHT

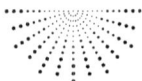

ALLEGRA

"*M*orning, Allegra," someone whispers. My heart kicks violently, ripping me out of sleep as I pull the blankets over my head like a shield.

Where am I? Who's with me? Am I in danger?

"You're safe," comes the voice I now recognize as Armando's. "Sorry, angel. I didn't mean to scare you."

I lower the blankets and blink, adjusting to the morning light illuminating the room. Kind hazel eyes meet mine, and a soft smile stretches across his handsome features. "I guess I'm still a little jumpy," I murmur, feeling heat crawl into my cheeks.

Armando frowns, but then offers a genuine, heart-stopping smile as he cups my cheek. "I hate that you ever had to wake up in fear. Never again, sweet girl."

I nod, fighting back the tears. I still can't believe this is real, that *he's* real. Last week I was sleeping in a closet, struggling to survive. And now? I'm in a cozy, warm bed with the sexiest man alive, and he's kind and gentle and knows how to speak directly to my soul.

It's too good to be true.

I peer over at Armando, sitting on the bed, fully dressed in a suit and tie. It strikes me how little I know about the man I've been living with. And now sleeping with.

"Going somewhere?" I ask, giving him a smile. I feel dumb for freaking out on him, but I know Armando isn't judging me.

"I have a meeting this morning." The answer rolls off his tongue easily enough, but something is off.

"What do you do? We haven't talked about it much," I hedge, sitting up in bed a bit.

Armando takes a deep breath, running a hand through his close-cropped, dark hair. "I wear a few hats at my job. Security, collections, stuff like that."

"But, like, where do you work? Security for who?"

He's quiet for a concerning amount of time before answering. "It's… complicated."

I frown, studying his face for any hint of why he's being so dodgy. "Okaaaay, well, where is your meeting?"

"Other side of town."

I roll my eyes, growing tired of his non-answers. "We're in New York City. Can you be more specific?"

"Sorry, old habit. Our meetings are private, so we're trained not to disclose that kind of information. Besides, I'll be back soon, so no need to worry." He smiles, but it doesn't reach his eyes.

Trained? Private? Complicated? Who is this man?

"I thought maybe I could come with you? Not to the meeting, but I could look for some work applications. I'm not going back to my uncle, so I figured I should start earning my–"

"No," Armando says forcefully, cutting me off.

I stare at him, blinking a few times to reconcile this man with the one who whispered such sweet, soothing things to me last night.

"I'm sorry. I'm not mad at you, sweetheart. I know that all must sound like bullshit," Armando says with a sigh. "I promise I'll tell you everything."

"Can you at least pick up some applications?"

Armando smiles, a real one this time, making me almost forget his strange reaction to my questions. "There's no need for you to work, angel. I make plenty for us to have anything and everything we need."

And just like that, my suspicions are back. Growing frustrated with this man, I cross my arms over my chest and narrow my eyes. "How am I supposed to trust that you'll provide when you won't even tell me what you do for a living? Plus, what if I want to work? It's not always about the money but about having a purpose. Or are you saying my only job is to wait around for you to come home?"

I'm out of breath by the time I'm done with my rant. My brain finally catches up to what my stupid mouth has been saying, and panic twists with regret in my stomach. In my experience, telling men off usually ends badly. Looking up at Armando, I can't read his expression, so I dip my head and curl my shoulders, bracing myself for his wrath.

"I'm sorry," he says, surprising the hell out of me. "I'm not trying to control or isolate you, Allegra." He reaches out, brushing his fingertips across my temple and cheek, urging me to look up at him. His multi-colored eyes reach deep into my soul, begging me to believe him. "I'll explain everything when I get back, okay? All I want is your safety and happiness."

I nod, letting Armando press his lips to my forehead. He tells me he'll be back soon, and I smile, but inside, I'm numb. Armando says he'll leave his card on the counter next to his iPad and I can order anything I need. Then he promises to bring back lunch. I can barely hear him over the alarm bells ringing in my ears.

My emotions are tied up in a massive knot in my belly, but I ignore them, choosing survival once more. I refuse to be taken advantage of again.

Once he's out of the bedroom, I spring into action, throwing on my old clothes and putting my hair up into a messy bun. Armando thinks I went back to sleep, but I sneak down the stairs and listen while he calls his driver and gives him the address he needs to be dropped off at.

Bingo.

Ten minutes later, I'm in the back of a cab hurtling toward the South Bronx on my first ever recon mission. I'm sure Armando didn't intend for me to order a taxi with his card and iPad, but I had to use the tools available.

I want to believe Armando. A less jaded version of me probably would. But I'll be damned if I'm going to trap myself in another helpless situation like I was with my uncle. If Armando won't tell me what his day job is, I'll have to find out for myself.

"You sure this is the right address, miss?" the cab driver shouts. He's nearly a hundred and fifty years old if I had to guess, and as far as I can tell, he can only hear out of one ear and see out of one eye.

"Yes," I reply, though my stomach churns as he comes to a stop in front of a seedy strip mall with most of the store-fronts abandoned.

The old man shrugs, apparently not overly concerned about fighting me on the matter. Fair enough. I don't know what I'd tell him, anyway.

Stepping out of the car, I quietly close the door and take stock of my surroundings. It looks like the only two businesses still open in this decrepit structure are a pizza place and a car repair shop, neither of which seems like an ideal meeting spot.

What the hell is your job, Armando?

"Easy now, we don't want any trouble," someone says from inside the repair shop.

"No trouble? Then why did you bring the muscle?" another man replies, his voice higher pitched and weaselly. It sounds familiar, but I can't place it.

"In case you decided to run your mouth again," Armando growls.

I stop dead in my tracks a few feet from the entrance to the shop. *Armando is the muscle? He said he was in security...*

A few other voices overlap, and I creep forward, peering through the glass door to see where the commotion is coming from. No one is in the front lobby, and I look around the door, trying to see if there is a bell or alarm that would trigger if I opened it. I don't see anything, so I take a chance and slip inside, closing the door behind me.

I take a calming breath, willing myself to stop shaking. I need to see who Armando is talking to and why they sound so familiar. The front desk is abandoned, but behind the reception area is a small hallway with a light at the end. The voices get louder the further down the hallway I venture, and I know I'm close.

"...any other customers lately?" the first man asks.

"What are you guys getting at?" the familiar voice whines. *Where have I heard it before?*

I slide along the wall until I reach the office at the end with the bright light on. Gathering up every scrap of courage, I peek through the crack in the door, and the air drains from my lungs when I finally see who's inside.

Aaron Charmicael.

My uncle's business partner.

I can't breathe, can't blink, can't feel my heart thumping in my chest as I absorb what this means. Has Armando known this whole time? Did he strike a deal with my uncle and Aaron? Oh, God, does he work for my uncle? Does he...

"Hey!" Aaron shouts, his brown eyes cutting across the room and landing on mine. "Who is that?"

I stumble backward, falling on my ass and banging my head against the narrow hallway wall. Jumping to my feet, I sway slightly at the sudden movement, then gasp when the office door is wrenched open.

Aaron is standing in front of me, a look of confusion plastered on his ugly mug. "Allegra?"

"Allegra!" Armando shouts at the same time.

"Who the fuck is Allegra?" the other man grumbles.

This can't be happening. It's worse than anything I could have imagined. Why am I so stupid? He said all the right things, and I fell right into his trap.

I back away with my hands up as I stumble out into the reception area. *Shit.* I don't have an escape plan. I didn't bring the iPad with me or the credit card. *What the hell was I thinking?*

"Your uncle has been looking for you everywhere," Aaron continues, following me into the main lobby. "He's pissed as hell, too. Shit, girl, I almost feel bad sending this text."

My eyes snap to his hands, where he hits his phone screen a few times and then shoves it into his pocket. "No, please–"

"You know her uncle?" Armando yells from down the hall.

Wouldn't he know that? Aren't they working together? What the fuck is going on, and how did I misread Armando so badly?

My thoughts spiral out of control as my heart hammers painfully in my chest. I try taking a breath, but it gets caught in my lungs, making me cough and nearly black out from lack of oxygen.

I need to leave. I need to get as far away from this fucking place, from these people, from this goddamn city as possible. I need to disappear and regroup.

Throwing my weight against the front door, I fall outside,

then scramble to my feet, somehow keeping my balance enough to run across the empty parking lot. I don't know where I'm going, only that I'll die if I stop.

"Allegra!" I hear Armando shout. "Allegra, wait! This isn't what you think. You're not safe here!"

No shit, Sherlock, I think bitterly. I'm not safe anywhere.

Despite my better judgment, I look over my shoulder at Armando, my heart splintering into a million pieces when his hazel eyes meet mine. Was anything he said real? Or did I swallow it up, hook, line, and sinker, like the idiot I am?

I'm jolted out of my pity party when I run smack dab into a solid structure. I nearly fall over, but someone grabs my arm, twisting it painfully as they pull me up.

"There you are, you ungrateful bitch." Fear strikes my heart at the sound of my uncle's voice, sending echoes of regret and panic through my body. "Get in the fuckin' car and don't make a sound. I haven't decided if I'm going to let you live or not."

I nod in defeat, letting him know I won't fight. I know I can't win.

He sneers at me, the sadistic sound coiling around my chest and squeezing until it feels like I'm breathing through a straw. Black circles dot the corners of my vision, and the last thing I see before I pass out is my uncle's mottled face, bulbous nose, and yellow-ish brown teeth as he widens his smirk.

CHAPTER NINE

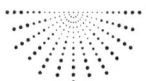

ARMANDO

A feral roar releases from somewhere deep in my chest. I grab the back of Aaron's collar, pulling him backward and slamming that motherfucker to the ground. He coughs and sputters for air, and I kick him in the ribs as I step over his body and sprint out the door.

"Allegra! Allegra, wait! This isn't what you think. You're not safe here!"

My beautiful, broken angel looks at me over her shoulder, searing me with a look I'll never forget. Pure betrayal bleeds from her gaze, a sorrow so deep, so heavy, I nearly collapse underneath its weight.

Still, I press on, needing to get her to safety. She can yell and curse and hit me all she wants as long as I know she's out of harm's way.

I pick up speed when I see a black SUV tear into the parking lot, and my vision grows red when a large man with a round, tomato-red face steps out. I open my mouth to scream at Allegra, but it's too late. The man grabs her and shoves her in the car before I can do anything.

I pump my legs, willing the adrenaline to push me to

superhuman speed as I chase after the vehicle. I'm aware of Valentino shouting my name in the distance, but nothing else matters. Allegra is in danger. I promised her my protection, promised she'd never have to go back to her uncle.

As the SUV turns a corner and gets lost in traffic, the realization finally sinks in. *I failed her.*

Black edges in on my vision as air saws in and out of my lungs. I reluctantly come to a stop before I pass out, doubling over to catch my breath.

"Armando," Valentino says from right next to me. I didn't realize he was so close. "What the fuck, man? Who was that? Why did you attack Aaron? Jesus Christ, are you okay?"

"I… Allegra… danger…" I huff, trying to put my thoughts into order. "No time."

"Breathe, buddy," Valentino says, patting my back. "That's the woman who has you all messed up in the head? She step out on you or something?"

Despite the exhaustion currently overtaking my body, I land a solid punch to his left arm. "Never speak ill of Allegra again," I growl.

Valentino holds up his hands and takes a step back. "I'm trying to figure out what the hell happened. Are we going after her?"

"We?" I ask, finally gaining enough strength to stand up straight. My hands shake as I pull out my phone, and honestly, I'm not sure who I'm going to call.

"Well, yeah," Valentino answers as if it's obvious. "You go, I go."

"I thought women were a *complication*."

"I'm not saying I understand your relationship, just that I have your back. I don't know that I'll ever love someone the way you obviously love Allegra, but that doesn't mean I don't want you to be happy. And I'm not okay with her being in danger."

"Maybe there's hope for you yet, kid," I grunt.

Valentino smirks, then returns to the task at hand. "What do we know?" he asks, getting right back into business mode.

"Allegra's uncle owns a strip club. Wants to force her to work there doing…" I trail off, not even wanting to think about the atrocious things my precious girl could be subjected to.

"Got it," Valentino pipes in. "And Aaron?"

"Shit." I curse, turn on my heel, and sprint back to the auto shop.

"Give a guy some warning next time," Valentino mutters as he follows close behind.

We burst through the door, and to my relief, Aaron is still squirming on the ground in the hallway. I nod at Valentino, who gathers up the pathetic man and ties his hands and feet. I don't have to tell him we're going to interrogate Aaron. He already knows and has his gun pressed against the fuck's temple, ready for questioning.

"How do you know Allegra?" I rasp, staring into Aaron's wide, terrified eyes. He's sweating profusely and bleeding slightly from a cut on his lip. It's a start, but nowhere near satisfying my appetite for revenge.

"I… Well, uh, I'm…"

Valentino digs the muzzle of his gun into Aaron's temple, prompting him to swallow thickly.

"Want to try that again?" I seethe.

"H-her uncle and I run a strip club. Teasers. Sh-she works there."

"What do you know about her uncle?"

"Tommy Brenshaw," he's quick to answer. "Real piece of shit, but a good eye for talent, if you know what I mean."

I sink my fist into his face, feeling somewhat better when his nose snaps. Blood pours down his face, the river of red matching my clouded vision.

"Jesus!" Aaron wails, wriggling in his restraints. "Is this why you came here? To ask about Allegra?"

"It is now," I answer, landing another blow.

"Armando," Valentino says, getting my attention. "We'll make him pay later. Save your wrath for her uncle."

I growl, not liking him telling me what to do.

"We have the info we need. The most important thing is getting your girl, remember?"

Nodding once, I knock Aaron out with a backhand to the head. Valentino tucks his gun away and motions toward our vehicle parked out back. I follow him, looking up directions for Teasers on the way.

"I've got the address here," I tell him when we get to the car.

"I texted Romeo and let him know what's up. He's sending Dante to meet us at Teasers."

Wrenching the driver's side door open, I startle my chauffeur, who takes one look at me and scrambles out of the way. Good man.

My hands shake as I take the wheel, and Valentino surprises me by clapping a hand over my shoulder. I'd punch him, but this car is too small for me to get enough momentum to do any damage.

"Whatever fear is pressing down on your chest and scrambling your thoughts? Don't give it power. You control this situation. We *will* get Allegra back. Got it?"

I nod, letting his words sink in. The tremble in my hands subsides enough for me to start the engine and peel out of the parking lot, heading north toward Teasers. Valentino is good under pressure, I'll give him that much.

Ignoring traffic laws and speed limits, I weave between lanes of cars at a break-neck pace. To his credit, Valentino doesn't say a single thing about my driving. He knows I'd just as soon unlock his door and shove him out if he tested me right now.

As soon as I see the hot pink sign for Teasers, I turn the wheel, jumping the curb as I pull up next to the decrepit structure with no windows. I'm about to tear the door off its hinges to get to my girl, but once again, Valentino rests his hand on my shoulder. Bold move, seeing as I'm ready to break necks first and ask questions later.

"You're in control," he repeats. "Don't let the anger and fear cloud your judgment."

"When did you become some new age guru?" I snap. "Every second we sit here is more time she's in danger."

"I'm trying to help," Valentino answers calmly. "I've been guided by rage before, and it nearly destroyed me. I don't want the same for you or Allegra."

"Fuck," I sigh, wiping a hand down my face.

"I've got your back. Let's be smart about this. We have the element of surprise. Tommy doesn't know we're associated with Allegra." I bob my head, listening to his plan. "I'll go in and conduct business as usual. We were supposed to talk to our mutual contacts in shitty establishments, and this fits the bill. I'll ask for Tommy. If he's half as smart as Aaron says he is, I'm sure he'll recognize the Di Salvo family when they show up. I'll distract him while you look for Allegra."

"What if they aren't here?"

"Then we'll figure it out. But something tells me Tommy will want to put your girl to work sooner rather than later."

I growl, the rush of adrenaline spiking once more. Valentino catches my eye, and we nod, knowing what needs to be done.

We get out of the car, and Valentino conceals his weapon as he straightens his suit. He heads to the front door while I hang back, sticking to the shadows as I make my way to the side entrance.

The door is propped open with a cracked cement block that doubles as an ashtray. I peer inside, noting the layout. It appears to be a prep room for the dancers and other workers, with lockers on one wall and a row of vanity mirrors on the other.

Luckily, it's early in the day. Hopefully, they'll be operating with a smaller staff until the sun goes down. I've learned from experience that darkness gives people permission to sin.

Keeping a hand on my gun, I step inside the building, ducking so my large frame can fit through the doorway. I'm immediately hit with the smell of cheap perfume and even cheaper alcohol. My angel deserves so much better than this.

"Yo, Tommy!" someone shouts. I freeze, every muscle pulled tight as I wait for the reply. "Tommy, you got some goon here to see you. You owe money again?"

"Stop runnin' your goddamn mouth, boy," the man I assume is Tommy grinds out. "Told you, I'm busy."

"He was very insistent, boss. Said something about the protection offered on this joint is in jeopardy. I thought we already had a couple bouncers, so I'm not sure what he's referring to, but–"

"Jesus H. Christ," Tommy mutters. "Fine."

Smart move on Valentino's part. While this strip club isn't under Di Salvo protection, it's a good bet that one of the local gangs struck up a deal with the business on this block. If Tommy thinks his club is in danger, he might take Valentino a bit more seriously. I just hope the Capo knows what he's doing.

There's a shuffling sound, followed by a gasp, and then Tommy hisses out, "If you move a fuckin' muscle, I'll stop being so nice. Understand?" A brief pause, followed by what sounds like a hand slapping against the wall. I hear a muffled cry that sends fury blazing through my veins.

Allegra.

Instinct takes over, and I reach for my gun, holding it at the ready as I fling open doors trying to find where that fuck put my angel. Valentino's words come back to me, reminding me to stay in control of my rage long enough to ensure Allegra's safety.

The sound of a thick curtain being pulled back gets my attention as I wander through the maze of private rooms presumably used for illegal goods and services. Noise from the front of the strip club grows louder, and I hear Tommy ask someone where the goon is.

It's time.

"Allegra," I call out, running down the hall where I heard her cry. Another muffled whimper stabs at my heart, but it's enough for me to lock onto the room she's in.

I kick down the door, which splinters far too easily, not that I'm complaining. Allegra's eyes widen in fear as she stares down the barrel of my gun, and then she ducks her head and turns away, trying to hide from me.

My heart rips in two at the sight of my sweet girl cowering in fear. The pain is amplified when I realize she's afraid of *me*.

I tuck my gun away and kneel in front of her, unsure where to begin. "I'm so sorry," I whisper, hovering my hands over her body.

She's tied to a chair with a rag covering her mouth to prevent her from speaking. My beautiful girl is trembling, her blue eyes bloodshot and rimmed in red.

I carefully untie and remove the cloth from her mouth, then get to work on her hands. "I'm so sorry," I repeat, rubbing the red, raw marks on her wrists from the rope burns. "I'm not going to hurt you," I whisper, sitting back on my heels to take her in. "I didn't know Aaron was associated with your uncle. I swear, Allegra. I would never…"

I clench my jaw so hard I'm positive I've cracked a tooth, but I can't help it. The thought of knowingly harming my woman, of sending her back to this disgusting establishment, has me ready to tear these walls down with my bare hands. I still might.

"Please trust me," I beg, leaning close enough to take her hand in mine. "I owe you answers, and I'll tell you everything when we get home. Right now, I need you to trust that I would never put you in danger. I would never hand you over to your uncle. I need you to trust me enough to let me get you out of here, okay?"

She hasn't said anything yet, and exhaustion weighs heavily on her shoulders. Tired, mournful eyes stare through me, like she doesn't know who or what to believe anymore.

"I'm so sorry, angel," I repeat. "We don't have much time." Without another word, I scoop her up in my arms.

Allegra curls up against me, burying her head between my neck and shoulder while silent sobs shake her body.

"I've got you," I whisper as I carry her through the hallway, dressing room, and out the side door to my car.

Dante is parked next to me, and his eyes immediately fall on Allegra. I give him a nod, and I know we're on the same page. *This is the most important thing to me. I have to go kill the man who hurt her, and you're going to watch over her.*

I open the back door to Dante's vehicle and gently set my girl down. Taking off my suit coat, I drape it over her body and then smooth her hair behind her ears, revealing more of her face to me. She has a few scrapes and smudges of dirt, but Allegra is still the most gorgeous creature I've ever laid eyes on.

"I'll be right back," I promise. "I'm going to make sure he never hurts you again."

Blue eyes meet mine, and she blinks once, letting me know she understands.

With Allegra safely out of the way, there's no need for subtlety as I rampage toward the front door of Teasers, tearing the fucking door off its hinges and throwing it behind me. Valentino is sitting with Tommy at the bar, and he grabs the man's right arm before he can pull out his gun. Tommy shouts as Valentino forces him into a standing position and twists his arm behind his back, holding him in place as I storm over.

Circling my fingers around his throat, I squeeze Tommy's neck until his eyes bulge and his face turns from red to purple. "I've killed many men, but this will be my most satisfying yet. Hell, putting an end to your pathetic life and the suffering you've caused might just make up for some of the other shit I've done."

Tommy sputters, trying to defend himself. I don't give him a chance.

"Enough. You don't deserve any last words. As much as I want to torture you and draw out your agony, I want to be with my Allegra more, so I'll make this quick."

Valentino steps out of the way as I shove Tommy to the ground with my hand still around his throat. I pull out my gun and rest the muzzle against his forehead, relishing in this man's final moments before pulling the trigger.

"Armando. *Armando*!"

I shake my head, then look up, realizing Valentino has been trying to get my attention.

"It's over. Go get your girl."

I blink a few times, then look down at the gory remains of Tommy, where my hand is still trying to choke him out. Releasing his neck, I stand and take a few steps back, reorienting to my surroundings.

"Hey. I got this," Valentino says as he hands me a damp rag. "We'll take care of the body. You go with Dante, and I'll get your car back to you."

I nod numbly, the words flowing over my head. "Clean up your hands and lose the shirt before going outside. Don't want Allegra seeing any more blood, yeah?"

This jolts me out of my stupor. "Right," I agree, getting to work on washing the blood from my hands. I unbutton my shirt, tossing it aside, along with my tie. Thankfully, my undershirt didn't get much on it, so I decide to leave it on. I'm not sure what Allegra thinks of me, and I don't want to crowd her space while half-naked.

I try taking deep breaths as I make my way back to Dante, but my mind is buzzing with what Allegra is going to say. She has every right to hate me. I'm a violent monster who deceived her about my line of work. It would make sense for her to not want anything to do with me after this.

When I see my angel curled up in the back of Dante's car, every doubt evaporates. I don't care if she never wants to see me again after this, so long as I get to hold her and make sure she gets somewhere safe.

I open the back door and slide in, not sure what to say or how to tell her I need to touch her before I go insane. Allegra shocks the hell out of me by crawling into my lap. I wrap her up in my arms, holding her close while Dante drives us through the city, back to my place.

"You're safe now," I whisper, absorbing her tears as she clings to me.

Allegra doesn't say anything. She simply nods and tries to get herself even closer, like she wants to dissolve into me. I don't mind. After today, I don't know that I'll ever let her out of my sight again.

CHAPTER TEN

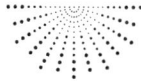

ALLEGRA

I can't let go of Armando. My arms are locked around his neck the entire ride back to his house, and I don't loosen my grip even when he shifts my weight to get out of the car. Armando carries me inside without missing a step, then collapses on the couch.

I immediately tuck my face into his shoulder, feeling raw and exposed. My head is spinning, my body aches, and my temples throb. I'm not sure what to think about anything or anyone. All I know is that Armando makes me feel safe. He rescued me. That has to count for something.

"Did he touch you?" Armando asks, his fingers skimming over my arms and neck, searching for wounds. "Are you hurt? I mean, Jesus, I know you're hurt. Fuck," he mutters. "What can I do? How can I make it better? God, Allegra, I failed you."

His voice cracks along with my heart. I peer up at him, seeing the worry, regret, and self loathing in his hazel eyes.

"Precious girl, I'm so sorry. Tell me how to fix this."

"The truth," I rasp, my voice scratchy from crying. "I want

to believe you," I add. "You're the only good thing that has ever happened to me."

"I should have been honest with you from the beginning. I see that now," he starts, tucking a few strands of hair behind my ear. "I was afraid I'd scare you off with my profession, and I wanted more time for you to get to know me, to see who I am away from what I do."

I nod slowly, trying to understand. "Do you work for my uncle?" I whisper, not strong enough to ask the question out loud.

"Fuck no," he answers forcefully. "Never."

The tight band squeezing my chest loosens. Armando's eyes burn with conviction, and I know he's telling me the truth.

"I work for the Mafia," he continues. My breath catches in my throat, and I blink at him a few times. "I'm an enforcer for the Di Salvo family."

"Security and collections," I say softly, repeating what he told me this morning.

"That's right. I use my strength to protect the family, secure assets, and take out the garbage." I nod, taking in his words. "We may be criminals, but we have a code. The Boss, Romeo, is very clear on that. No women, no children, no human trafficking."

The longer I stare into the brutally honest eyes of the man I love, the more my heart softens. I can see him breaking apart, crumbling at the thought of losing me.

Armando strokes my cheek, his touch achingly tender. "Remember when you asked me why I took you in and gave you a place to stay?" I nod, furrowing my brow. "I was nothing more than a dirty street rat. I got sick of being shuffled around foster families and group homes, so I ran away with my only friend, Leif. We did what we had to do to survive."

"Oh my god," I murmur, stunned by his confession. I would never have guessed the man with a home theater who always dresses in a suit was homeless as a teen.

"Leif found a way out through the military. I knew I couldn't follow him. Never could picture myself as a soldier, but I guess I needed to find a different leader to follow."

The corner of Armando's lip twitches, and I somehow know it's a joke he must share with his childhood friend. I get the strangest urge to meet him and thank him for having my man's back.

"Romeo caught me stealing from one of the Di Salvo warehouses," Armando goes on. "I thought he was going to shoot me, but instead, he offered me a job and a place to live. I was suspicious as hell, but smart enough to realize I'd never have an opportunity like that again. I know it's a lot to process, Allegra. I understand if you don't want to see me anymore. I'll leave you alone if that's what you–"

"Don't leave me," I whimper, my heart squeezing painfully in my chest. The words come spilling out of my mouth before I can think them through, but I don't regret it.

Armando cups my face, wiping away my tears with the pads of his thumbs. "If you want me, I'm yours, Allegra. But you have to say it. Tell me you can forgive me for failing you."

Leaning forward, I rest my forehead on his. "I forgive you for not being honest, though I understand why you did what you did." The tension drain from Armando's muscles, like he's finally able to breathe for the first time all day. "You didn't fail me, though."

"I did," he counters. "I failed to protect you. I promised your uncle would never harm you again, but…" He shakes his head in disgust, but I stop the motion with a kiss to his forehead. This man is unraveling before me, destroyed at the thought of anything bad happening to me under his watch.

"I followed you," I admit. "I overheard the address you told your driver and ordered a cab with the iPad. It was my fault, Armando. I put myself in danger because I didn't trust you."

"No, sweet girl. None of this is your fault. I didn't give you a reason to trust me."

"You gave me a thousand little reasons. I let my fear take over and jumped to the worst conclusion."

Armando combs his fingers through my hair, letting his fingers trail down my spine. "You have been through a lot of trauma, Allegra. It makes sense that you wouldn't trust easily. I should have known you would see me for me. I should never have given you a reason to doubt me in the first place."

My incredibly gentle yet fierce protector closes the distance between us, kissing me softly, taking his time to taste me and explore my mouth. It's so sweet and tender I feel like I might cry.

"Armando," I breathe, feeling our connection once more.

There's no room for doubt when he's pouring his heart and soul into every touch, every whispered word, every kiss. I need him in the most primal way, need him to take control and show me how perfect we are together.

"Angel," he murmurs, his lips brushing against the shell of my ear. "Do you need something from me?"

"Please…" I whimper, pressing my body against his and trailing my hands up his chest. God, I never thought I'd see him again, let alone touch him. I need more.

"I've got you, sweet girl. I know what you need," he murmurs.

Armando gives me one last kiss and stands from the couch. Before I can protest, he lifts me in his arms and carries me toward the bathroom, kissing me the whole way there.

As soon as he sets me down, he turns on the water in the

shower, testing its warmth. When he's satisfied, he turns, his dark eyes nearly feral as they roam over my body. Slowly, he slides his hands up my torso beneath my shirt. He gently pulls it off, followed by my bra and jeans.

When I'm in just my panties, he growls and cups my pussy, rubbing me through the thin material. "I feel your heat, angel. Feel how much you need this."

I nod, gasping when Armando fists the fabric and rips it off my body. His mouth covers mine, swallowing my breath in a devastating kiss. We break apart only so he can strip down.

He helps me into the shower once we're both naked, his fingertips following the streams of water as they pour over my shoulders, my breasts, my torso, my hips, and finally my throbbing pussy. I moan as his knuckles barely graze my mound before continuing down my inner thighs.

Armando's other hand wraps around the back of my neck, pulling me in for a punishing kiss. I open up for him, needing to taste and touch and feel him everywhere. He tugs my hair, pulling my head back so he can deepen the kiss. Two fingers dip into my slit and circle my little bundle of nerves in slow, steady strokes.

I grip his biceps, digging in my nails as one finger pushes into my entrance, then two. Armando thrusts his large digits in and out of me, slowly at first, and then faster, faster, faster, grinding his heel down on my clit all while devouring my lips.

Breaking the kiss, I bury my face in between his neck and shoulder as I cry out. I'm *right* there, so close to my much-needed release. He keeps pumping his fingers, twisting and curling them up to rub against my G-spot. Again, again, once more time…

Suddenly, his hand is gone. I nearly fall over at the loss of him, but I regain my composure and glare at him. Armando just grins, which makes my pussy clench.

"Not yet. Patience, sweetheart," he rasps.

With that, he spins me around, my back to his front, and starts massaging me everywhere. His large, calloused hands squeeze my breasts, hips, and my soft, round belly I've always been a little self-conscious about. Armando has made it clear he loves every inch of me.

His hands trail lower, teasing my pussy lips. My clit throbs in time with my heartbeat, begging him to do something about the unbearable ache he's created.

"Armando…" I moan, wriggling my hips to get him to touch me where I need him most.

"Not yet," he murmurs again, licking the shell of my ear before trailing kisses down my neck and shoulder.

His hard cock digs into my ass, so I wiggle a bit more until I feel his length nestle between my cheeks. Armando groans and rotates his hips, grinding his thick shaft against my ass.

"God, please, Armando," I beg. My legs shake, and I lean forward to brace myself against the wall.

A low growl rises from deep in Armando's chest, and the sound vibrates through me, nearly making me come on the spot. He grips my left leg under my knee and lifts it so my foot is resting on a bench I didn't notice before in the corner of the shower.

"That's it. Fuck, I love it when you're spread out for me." He continues touching every inch of me, caressing my thighs and widening my stance.

Armando gives me a satisfied grunt, which makes me giggle. My laughter is cut off when his cock slides along my slit. He taps my clit, nearly sending me over the edge. I'm so damn sensitive and ready to come, I think I might die if he doesn't get inside me soon.

"I've got you, Allegra," he murmurs, lining himself up with my entrance.

I'm expecting him to thrust inside me and fuck me hard. I know he's as desperate for me as I am for him. But Armando slowly inches inside, prolonging the sweet pain deep in my core. He grips my hips, holding me in place as he stretches me open. I hold my breath as he slides home, hitting the very end of me.

"You feel so damn good," he murmurs, more to himself than me.

Armando pulls out just as slowly, making me whine. I open my mouth to tell him to fuck me already, but then he slams his thick dick all the way inside, making me come instantly.

He wraps his arms around me, holding me up as I spasm around his cock. He fucks me through it, hammering into me over and over as I continue to convulse and cry out his name. He grips the inner thigh of my leg that's propped up, spreading me wider and angling my hips so he's hitting that special spot with every thrust.

"Y-y-yesss…" I hiss as I pound my fist against the wall and throw my head back against his shoulder.

Armando wraps his hand around my throat, keeping my head tilted back as he splits me open with his dick. "So tight for me, love," he grits.

I whimper as another orgasm rushes to the surface. He must sense it, too. He keeps a firm grip on my neck, which is hot as fuck, and then trails his other hand down my body, circling and pinching my clit.

My orgasm slams into me, hard and fast, ripping a scream from my lips. Armando growls and ruts into me, rubbing furious circles over my swollen, pulsing clit. A painful, delicious pleasure takes over every part of my body as I come again for him, sobbing his name.

Armando pulls out and spins me around, crashing his lips down on mine as he lifts me and spears me with his cock. I wrap my legs around his hips and hang on for dear life as he pins me to the wall and fucks me like a man possessed.

"Mine, mine, fucking *mine*. Say it, Allegra. Tell me."

"Y-yours," I whisper, my voice scratchy from screaming his name.

"Louder," he growls.

"I'm yours!" I cry out, writhing in his arms.

Armando roars and bites my shoulder as he comes, marking me, claiming me, fucking me raw. I gasp and open my mouth in a silent scream, my entire body pulsing, tensing, stretching… and then collapsing in on itself as my orgasm ravishes me from the inside out.

I swear I feel Armando come again, shooting his cum deep inside me in forceful bursts.

I drag air into my lungs in short breaths, trembling in Armando's arms as he keeps me pinned to the wall. I comb my fingers through his hair while he nuzzles into my shoulder, kissing over the spot where he bit me.

Eventually, he sets me on my feet, grabbing the body wash and massaging it all over my skin. I lean against him, letting him hold me up as the water sluices down my back, carrying the soapy suds with it.

"I love you," he murmurs, circling his arms around my back. "I love you so much it hurts. I love every single thing about you, and I've wanted to tell you the moment you leaped into my arms that first day."

My heart bursts with so many emotions as I cling to this incredible man. "I love you too," I squeak.

Armando stills, then peels me off of his chest. "Say it again," he commands, his magical eyes never leaving mine.

"I love you, Armando. You make me feel confident and sexy, and most of all, safe."

"Even after today?" he asks softly.

"Always. I know you'll come for me if I'm ever in danger. I know you'll fight for me when I need it. I know you'll protect me no matter the cost."

Armando nods, cupping my neck and pressing his lips to my forehead. "Love you with my whole goddamn heart, angel."

With one last kiss, Armando shuts off the water and wraps me in a fluffy towel, drying every inch of me before scooping me into his arms. I relax in his embrace, half asleep by the time he tucks me into bed and crawls in behind me, curling his body around mine.

We have more to talk about, but right now, all is right in my world.

CHAPTER ELEVEN

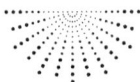

ARMANDO

*I*t was almost impossible to leave Allegra this morning, but Romeo called a meeting. After everything that went down yesterday, including an unsanctioned execution and clean up, I knew I couldn't decline.

My girl said she understood, and even wanted me to pass along her apologies, which of course, I won't. It's entirely too sweet. Then again, that's my angel. Tender-hearted, despite everything she's been through. And she said she loves me. How fucking crazy is that? I still can't believe it.

"Yo, I'm glad you got your girl home safe, but you gotta wipe that dopey look off your face, man. It's freaking me out," Valentino whines.

"He's always been dopey," Dante quips. His smirk isn't nearly as potent as before. Probably because there's less of a bite. After entrusting my Allegra to his care, there's an unspoken bond between us.

"And how is Allegra? Should I send the doctor over?" Romeo asks.

"Thank you, but that won't be necessary. She's recovering fine. Still shaken up, but then again, so am I."

Valentino scoffs, but Romeo nods. "I'm glad she's resting," he says, crossing his arms over his chest the way he does at the end of most meetings. "I know you're even more anxious than usual to get out of here, so I won't keep you much longer. We do, however, have some news about the Colombos."

At this, every man sits up straight, including myself. Valentino and I didn't have much success in gathering intel yesterday, but apparently, Romeo and Dante had better luck.

Romeo cuts a glance to Dante, who stands and takes the lead.

"A large sum of money was recently transferred from one of the Colombo's offshore accounts to a known black-market weapons dealer. A few days later, a shipment of explosives, guns, and ammo was intercepted and redirected to New York City. We don't know where exactly it ended up, but it's no coincidence."

"They're stockpiling," I grunt.

"Enough for a war," Romeo finishes for me. "We have our own reserves, but let's hope it doesn't come to that."

The room is silent, the air still as the realization of war sets in.

"Our number one priority is finding the stockpile of weapons. Without that to fall back on, we might be able to get the upper hand and mitigate lives lost," Dante rattles off. I'm sure he has plans on plans and three backup plans for each additional plan, but I'm not in the headspace to go over the minutia.

"Armando and I will hit the streets again, hopefully with more luck this time," Valentino says.

I nod in agreement, though I'm hoping to see Allegra before going on another assignment. As if reading my thoughts, Romeo stands from his chair and interjects.

"Tomorrow. For today, rest. We have many battles ahead of us, men."

"Yes, Boss."

"Aye, Boss."

"We're with you, Boss," all three of us say in unison.

He dismisses us, and I bolt out of his office, not bothering to say a single word to anyone else. Tensions have been high between the two families for a long time, but now it seems war is imminent. It makes every moment with Allegra that much more precious.

Hopping in my car, I rev the engine and get the fuck out of there, hitting the road at nearly twenty over the speed limit. With the timing of everything, I'm more positive than ever I made the right decision this morning to stop by the jewelry store.

I don't know jack shit about rings, but luckily for me, Leif recently married the love of his life. They were both all too happy to help me pick out the perfect ring for my angel. Now I just need to figure out a way to ask her.

As soon as I step inside my house, my eyes are drawn to Allegra. She's lounging on the couch, scrolling through the iPad.

A smile takes over her delicate features when she sees me. "You're home," she says excitedly, patting the seat next to her.

"So are you," I reply, sitting down and drawing her into my arms.

"Really? I mean, I was hoping, but just in case, I was looking at apartments…"

"I want you here with me," I tell her, capturing her blue eyes and letting her see how much I mean it. "I don't think I'll ever be able to sleep without you by my side."

"Are you sure? Everything happened so fast between us, and if you need space–"

Unable to listen to any more of her doubts, I untangle myself from Allegra and slide off the couch, kneeling on one knee in front of her. She blinks down at me, a look of shock and disbelief written across her face. I hope it's good shock, but I can't be sure.

"I never want space from you," I rush to say. "Knew you were it for me as soon as I held you. It was my mission to protect you, and even though I let you down once, I'd like to apply for the job full-time. Forever."

I take out the little velvet box, opening it to reveal a white-gold ring with a princess-cut diamond in the center, surrounded by light blue sapphires that match her eyes.

"Armando… oh my god," she breathes, her eyes filling with tears.

Shit. "It's too much," I mutter to myself. "I'll take it back. We'll get something else. Whatever you want. One for each finger. We can–"

"Armando," she says again, snapping me out of my spiral. A smile curls up one side of her lips, and the sparkle has returned to her beautiful eyes. "It's beautiful. I can't believe you want to keep me."

I take her left hand and slide the ring on her finger, not giving her a chance to turn me down. "I thought I made that clear," I tell her, standing and caging her in with my body. "You're perfect, Allegra. My sweet girl. Yes, things happened very fast between us, but what we have is real. You feel it too, right?" She nods, easing the tension in my shoulders. "So what do you say?"

"You didn't really ask, you know," she sasses, nibbling on her bottom lip.

"Allegra. My strong, brave, brilliant, precious girl. Will you do me the honor of being my wife?"

A devious spark flashes in her eyes. Christ, I'm going to love bringing more of that out.

"Yes, sir," she purrs, looping her arms around my neck and pulling me down for a kiss. I get lost in everything she has to offer, and my hands wander over her body, massaging her flesh as we devour each other.

Soon, I need more. More access to her creamy skin and tight little pussy. More kisses, more moans, more everything. Unable to wait another second, I lift Allegra in my arms, making her gasp.

"Need to show my fiancée exactly how good I'm going to make her feel every single day," I grunt before blazing a trail of kisses up her neck.

"Yes, please," she pants, tightening her thighs around me as I carry her upstairs and into our bedroom.

As soon as the door clicks shut, I press her back against the wall with the weight of my body and slam my mouth over hers, thrusting my tongue in between her lips so I can have another taste. She moans softly for me, then loudly as I tangle my fingers in her long hair and angle her head to deepen the kiss. A sharp thread of desire slices through me when her teeth sink into my bottom lip.

"God, Allegra," I groan, kissing down her neck and nipping at her pulse point.

Her deft little fingers are already working at my shirt, and soon it's discarded on the floor behind me. Then she attacks my belt, followed by the button and zipper of my pants. She shoves her hand into my boxer briefs and pulls out my throbbing cock, giving it a rough stroke that nearly brings me to my knees.

I cage her in with a hand on the wall beside her head as she pumps my massive erection with both hands. I squeeze my eyes shut and concentrate on how the soft skin of her hands glides up and down my shaft, teasing me with each stroke. I thrust my hips and shove my dick deeper into her tight grip. Again and again, we work together to jerk me off.

I should probably be upset that I'm going to come so soon, but I know I'll be hard for her all fucking night, no matter what.

My balls draw up tight as she swirls the pad of her thumb over the tip of my cock while her other hand squeezes the base. The fucker jumps in her hands and swells up, almost ready to go off…

And then she's not touching me.

My eyes snap open and I look down to see Allegra on her knees for me, tugging my pants and boxer briefs all the way down so they pool at my ankles.

"Jesus," I grunt, unable to stop the first spurts of cum from leaking out of me.

Allegra licks the drops off of the tip of my dick, massaging the little slit there and making my knees shake. I watch in awe as her pink tongue darts out and tickles the underside of my cock from tip to base. I ball my hands into fists on the wall and hold on to my release as long as I can.

She licks me up and down and then presses a kiss to my balls, making me growl. Allegra pulls back and stares up at me, her blue irises practically swallowed whole by her dilated pupils.

"You like that? Like my big fucking cock?"

She nods enthusiastically and bites her bottom lip. "Yes, sir."

"Show me," I grunt, barely hanging on.

Her nostrils flare and her eyes go wide with the challenge. Goddamn, what that does to me. Allegra unhinges her jaw and takes me into her hot, wet little mouth, sucking me down with the same frenzied need building deep inside me.

She sets a relentless pace, bobbing her head up and down my thick dick, taking more of me with each downward stroke. I pound my balled-up fist on the wall when she swirls her tongue over a particularly sensitive vein. The little siren does it again and again, making me tremble.

Her nails rake down the back of my thighs and I almost collapse from the sudden urgent need for release. Not like this, though. It was supposed to be about her.

With an incredible amount of self-restraint I didn't know I had, I peel Allegra off my painfully hard cock and pull her up, tilting her head back with the hand in her hair. My lips claim hers in a wild kiss.

I growl and nip at her lips, her chin, her neck, and then rest my forehead on hers, panting for air. Allegra looks disheveled, her hair sticking out, her cheeks stained red, her lips swollen. She closes her eyes and leans against the wall while I gaze at her.

One word echoes in my head, beats in my heart, and swims in my veins.

More. More. More.

I strip off what little clothes I have left and practically tear Allegra's clothes off her.

"Hey!" she shrieks and giggles.

"Need you," I grunt, biting and kissing her again.

She gasps when I lift her into my arms, automatically wrapping her legs around my waist as I carry her to the bed.

"I ache for you," she whispers against my lips.

It's more than I can take.

I stand in front of the bed with her in my arms and lick my way up and down her slender throat. Fuck, I swear I can feel her skin buzzing underneath my tongue.

Allegra lowers her head and kisses me with fire and fury. Her pussy grinds against my abs, which instinctively flex as she rubs her juices into my skin. Jesus, I don't think I'm going to make it the two steps to the bed.

I lift Allegra and reposition my hips slightly before sinking into her tight, perfect little pussy.

"Oh, god," she moans. "More, sir. Please…"

I cut her off with a kiss, needing to taste her while I fuck her mid-air. My hands wrap around her thighs as I lift and drop her sexy fucking body on my cock again and again.

"Just gotta take the edge off, Allegra. Just a little longer," I grunt.

She whimpers and buries her face into the side of my neck, rocking her hips in rhythm with my thrusts. I feel her tighten around me, her cunt soaking me and pulling me deeper inside her. Right before she reaches her climax, I toss her on the bed and climb on top of her, entering that tight little hole in one hard thrust.

"Armando!" she screams, her back bowing off of the bed.

I hold myself up on one forearm beside her head, while my other hand slides down the dips and curves of her body. I squeeze her breast and massaging her luscious hips before finally gripping her ass and angling her hips so my rough strokes hit her most sensitive spot every time.

I lick the sweat from between her full, tempting breasts, and then suck on her nipples until Allegra comes so perfectly for me, trembling and moaning my name over and over. She's still writhing beneath me as I roll us over, flipping our positions, my dick still deep inside her pussy.

"Fuck," I whisper to myself. Seeing her like this has me on edge.

She pushes herself up on shaky arms and tosses her head back as she groans and adjusts to our new position. Her hips move slightly to the side, which makes her pussy flutter and suck me in. Allegra gasps and does it again, unaware of the exquisite torture she's putting me through.

Then she opens her eyes, searing me with her crystal blue gaze.

"Ride my hard as fuck cock, Allegra. And tell me how much you love it," I growl before smacking her ass.

Her eyes grow dark as she lifts herself on her knees slowly, so fucking slowly, dragging her quivering pussy up my shaft one agonizing inch at a time. When just the tip is inside her, she flashes me a devious smirk and drops down on me, swiveling her hips and grinding that sweet cunt into the base of my cock. I roar as her nails tear into my skin, bucking my hips to meet her thrust for thrust.

"You feel so good, sir," she moans. "You're so deep like this. I love it. I love your cock."

"Goddamn, Allegra," I grunt, flexing my hips as she continues to ride me.

She lets out a throaty moan that has me ready to burst. Then she sits up and grabs her tits, squeezing them hard. Jesus, I feel her pussy walls contract each time she pinches her berry-pink nipples.

My goddess rolls her body and kneads her breasts, giving me the sexiest show of my goddamn life. I hold her hips in place and fuck up into her so hard she falls forward onto my chest, catching herself with a hand on either side of my head. Those delicious tits dangle in front of me, so I take the opportunity to suck on them while gripping her ass, continuing my hard thrusts into her tight, hot cunt.

Allegra lets out sexy little whimpers each time I hit the end of her. Her muscles tighten, her skin dripping with sweat, and her entire body shakes with the effort of holding back her orgasm.

"Don't come yet, angel. Don't you dare come yet," I whisper into her neck before kissing her there.

"Please, sir," she moans. "I n-need it."

I spank her, making us both cry out with the sensation. Another swift smack to the ass has her pussy pulsing around me, almost setting me off.

"Not yet," I warn.

"Oh god, oh my god, please, sir, please, fuck, please…"

I thrust into her, holding her in place and spearing her with my cock. I can feel my orgasm crawling down my spine with each stroke. Allegra gasps for air, her eyes shining with tears as she pushes her climax back, fighting off every instinct in her curvy little body. It's so fucking beautiful, the way she controls herself for me.

I lift her all the way off me and then slam her down one last time. "Come for me, Allegra. Come for me right the fuck now," I grit.

She screams her release as her arms give out. I hold her tightly against me, my ridged cock buried to the hilt as the wild throb of her orgasm travels the length of my shaft. The sensation is incredible, like nothing I've ever felt.

I empty myself inside her as Allegra keeps coming around me, our joined climax wringing out every ounce of pleasure from our bodies. She holds her breath as deep spasms tremor through her muscles, milking me dry.

I kiss her softly as each shudder passes through her, pressing my lips to her chin, cheek, nose, and forehead.

Allegra snuggles deeper into me and tucks her head under my chin. I chuckle softly as she curls up on my chest like a cat. She even purrs like one, too.

I gather her left hand in mine, lifting it to my lips and kissing her ring. It looks perfect on her little finger.

"I love it," she whispers, peering up at me. "I love *you*."

"Love you so fucking much, angel."

She smiles at me, then yawns adorably.

"Get some sleep, love," I say softly. "I'll be right here, always."

"Always," she repeats as she drifts off.

Her confidence in me, even after the last twenty-four hours, is humbling. I'll spend the rest of my life making sure she never regrets trusting me that first day she ran into my arms.

EPILOGUE

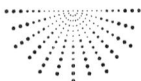

ALLEGRA

"**G**o set these on the table and then come back for your next assignment," I tell Aaron, our five year old. He beams up at me as he takes the napkins, his eyes the same magical hazel color as his father's. I watch Aaron's chubby little legs carry him into the dining room, where everything is ready for Armando's birthday dinner when he comes home.

Something tugs on the hem of my apron, and I look down to see little Alison, our mischievous three year old, with a marker in one hand and a fistful of my apron fabric in her other hand.

"And what are you doing, little miss?" I ask as I scoop her up into my arms. Little red ringlets bounce in front of her eyes, and I blow them out of her face, making my daughter giggle.

She shows me the marker in her hand, which thankfully still has the cap on, and grins like she just won a prize.

"Yes, I see. Have you been convincing your brother to get things for you that you know you aren't supposed to have?

Alison's eyes grow wide, and even at such a young age,

she's learned to pretend to be innocent. It's a good thing she's a terrible liar. It'll keep her out of trouble for a little bit longer, anyway.

"What now?" Aaron asks as he bounces into the kitchen and stands next to me.

"How about giving me a hug?" Armando says as he strides into the room.

"Dad!" Aaron squeals, racing into his father's arms. "Happy birthday!"

Armando tosses our rowdy boy in the air and catches him, spinning him around the room before setting him back down and turning his attention to me.

"Hey, beautiful," he murmurs, pressing his lips to my temple. "Missed you."

I smile up at my husband, knowing he means every word. Even though Armando has scaled back on the number of assignments he takes, the days he has to go into work are always long. He always makes up for it, though. By the way his hand is lingering on my lower back, I know he's thinking the same thing.

"Missed you, too," I tell him, leaning in for a kiss. My husband slides his hand against the side of my neck, holding me close as his lips claim mine. We've been married for over six years now, but each kiss is just as life-giving as the first one.

"Dad!" Alison shouts right in our faces. I almost forgot she was propped up on my hip.

Armando chuckles, breaking our kiss. "Ali," he says in the same tone, booping her nose. She bursts into a round of giggles, which only intensify when Armando takes her from me and starts tickling her round little belly.

"Alright, kids," I say, looking between Aaron and Alison. "Go wash up for dinner." They do as I say, and Armando turns to head that way as well. I grab him by his sleeve and pull him into me. "Not you," I tell him with a smirk. "I'm not done with you yet."

Armando grins wickedly, circling his arms around me and fusing his lips to mine. I open up for my man, savoring his kiss, the way his tongue glides against mine in steady strokes. I'm vaguely aware of being lifted and set down on the counter, my thighs spreading so my husband can stand between them.

"And how can I be of service, my sexy wife?" he purrs into the side of my neck. "Need me to kiss you some more?" I nod, sighing when Armando licks his way up and down my slender column. "Need me to taste you, angel? Need me inside you?"

"Yes," I hiss, looping my arms around his neck and pulling him down for more.

"God, Allegra," he groans.

Right as he's about to devour me, the kids come back.

"Ew," Aaron states as he walks past us. Armando laughs, tucking my hair behind my ear and placing a kiss on my forehead before helping me off the counter.

"Aaron, why don't you tell your dad what we made for dinner?" I ask, still flushed from that kiss.

"You made dinner?" Armando asks our son. Aaron holds out his hand and leads his dad around the table, showing off the dishes we made for his special birthday meal.

"Mom helped a little," he says, throwing me a bone. I roll my eyes as Armando stifles a laugh. I don't mind.

Aaron has been really into cooking lately, and I love encouraging that in him. It's worth the stacks of dishes in the sink and the disaster zone that is the rest of the kitchen to see how much pride he has showing off the lasagna and homemade bread sticks.

I get Alison settled in her booster seat at the table, then take my place next to my husband while he serves everyone.

"This is incredible," he says after everyone has started.

"I got the recipe from Thalia," I tell him with a grin.

"The very same recipe that convinced you to stay with me all those years ago," he says softly.

"Yes, if it weren't for the lasagna, I would have been out of there," I tease.

"I'm thankful you stayed, angel," my sweet husband whispers, resting his hand on my thigh underneath the table.

"Me, too. Happy birthday, love."

"Love you with my whole heart, Allegra. Thank you for bringing so much joy to my life, not just today, but every day. You make life worth living."

I swallow through the tears clogging my throat and manage to give Armando a smile. "There you go again, always saying the perfect thing."

"I'm trying, angel. Anything I can do to keep you by my side."

"Anything?" I ask, raising an eyebrow in challenge. "I might have a few ideas for later…"

Armando's eyes turn dark, and a rush of liquid heat trickles down my spine.

"…And then uncle Romeo let us practice throwing darts and a picture of an old, wrinkly man in a suit!" Aaron says excitedly, pulling us out of the moment.

"He let you throw darts?" I ask in shock, looking over at my son. Aaron nods enthusiastically and mimics throwing a dart.

Armando chuckles, and I glare at him. He raises his hands in surrender, though he still has a grin plastered on his face. "I'll talk to him about letting the kids play with pointy objects," he promises, though he gives Aaron a wink.

Truthfully, I know Romeo, Dante, and Valentino love their families as well, and would never harm our kids. Still, someone has to keep these guys in check every once in a while.

Armando laces his fingers through mine once more, resting our joined hands in his lap. We listen to our kids tell us about their day, and I soak up everything about this moment. I have a family filled with love, two kids who laugh and smile all the time, and the sweetest husband in the world, despite his less-than normal career.

I had no idea life could be this good. When I look over at Armando, his hazel eyes meet mine, a spark of love and understanding buried deep inside. I know my husband is thinking the exact same thing.

I can't wait to see what our future holds.

* * *

THE END
Curious about Valentino? Get his story here!

Want to know more about Leif & HEA? Check out Still a Warrior!

Want more mafia goodness?
Check out the Moscatelli Crime Family!

ABOUT THE AUTHOR

Cameron Hart is a USA Today bestselling author of contemporary romance. She writes books with lots of heat, plenty of sweet, and just enough drama to keep things interesting.

Want to meet me? Check out events and book signings I'll be attending across the US: https://www.cameronhart.net/meet-me-in-person/

Sign up for my newsletter and get a free novella!

f **◎** **ⓐ** **BB** **ⓖ** **♪**

ALSO BY CAMERON HART

Check out my other popular series and books!

Mafia, MC, & Bodyguard Romance:

Moscatelli Crime Family Series

Di Salvo Crime Family Series

Chaos MC series

Savage Ride

Ace

Watchdog Protection, Inc.

Mountain Man Romance:

Men of Blackthorne Mountain Series

Bear's Tooth Mountain Men Series

Curvy Girl Romance:

Curvy Temptations Boxset

Infinity

Claiming His Babygirl

Secret Temptations Boxset

At First Sight

Designed by Fate

My Heart & Soul

Finding Her Strength

1012 Curvy Way

Office Romance:

Boss Me Series

Beastly Brute

Executive Rule

Cowboy & Small Town Romance:

Roped in by Love Series

Sequoia Stud Farm

Small Town Love Boxset

Where I Belong

Seducing Sophia

Take Me Home

Forbidden Romance:

Secret Obsession

Secret Protector

Secret Desire

Holiday Romance:

Adored by Landon

Unwrapping His Package

Coming Down Her Chimney

His Christmas Angel

Hungry for Owen

Snow & Her Seven White Lies

Accidental Valentine

For Richer or Poorer

Printed in Dunstable, United Kingdom